ZEPPY RILEY

To Lee & Elaine
All my Best...
Joy

ZEPPY RILEY

HOY VAN HORN

TATE PUBLISHING
AND ENTERPRISES, LLC

Zeppy Riley
Copyright © 2014 by Hoy Van Horn. All rights reserved.

No part of this publication may be reproduced, stored in a retrieval system or transmitted in any way by any means, electronic, mechanical, photocopy, recording or otherwise without the prior permission of the author except as provided by USA copyright law.

This novel is a work of fiction. Names, descriptions, entities, and incidents included in the story are products of the author's imagination. Any resemblance to actual persons, events, and entities is entirely coincidental.

The opinions expressed by the author are not necessarily those of Tate Publishing, LLC.

Published by Tate Publishing & Enterprises, LLC
127 E. Trade Center Terrace | Mustang, Oklahoma 73064 USA
1.888.361.9473 | www.tatepublishing.com

Tate Publishing is committed to excellence in the publishing industry. The company reflects the philosophy established by the founders, based on Psalm 68:11,
"The Lord gave the word and great was the company of those who published it."

Book design copyright © 2014 by Tate Publishing, LLC. All rights reserved.
Cover design by Allen Jomoc
Interior design by Jomar Ouano

Published in the United States of America

ISBN: 978-1-62994-932-1
1. Fiction / General
2. Fiction / Dystopian
14.01.02

It's easier to build strong children than to repair broken men.

—Frederick Douglass

DEDICATION

For Judy, with love…H. V.

CHAPTER 1

Jonathon Van Lorne worked as a security supervisor at the Stockton Nuclear Power Plant. It was said that the further you went down Liberty Lane in Stockton, Pennsylvania, the meaner and more belligerent the people were. Jon lived in the last house on a no-outlet lane without a cul-de-sac. Jon had his own softball team. The team was called the Alley Ratts, who were sponsored by a local bar named "Rocky's." Rocky's Alley Ratts were undefeated for the last four seasons because Jon, who was the leader of the "Ratt Pack" and the manager of the team, demanded that they win. No excuses. The team would meet at Rocky's after every game to celebrate each obvious win.

Jock "Judge" Clydesdale, who was the slugger on the team, known as Judge because his father was a justice appointed to the Supreme Court, said to Jon, "It's too bad that my father disappeared after his divorce from my mom, because he could afford to buy some new equipment and uniforms."

"Yeah!" said Jon, gasping for air. "These nasty shirts with Rocky's Alley Ratts on the back are disgusting, although Rocky said he may get us some new ones."

Sparky laughed out load and said, "Fat chance of that happening. Rocky is still paying child support for his six kids to his three ex-wives who are very demanding."

Samuel "Sparky" Simcox lived just two doors from Jon on Liberty Lane in a story and a half, Cape-Cod–style home, with his wife Laura and his two highly intelligent twin sons. Sparky was so happy to be living on Liberty Lane because his former residence was too small and his two boys were in high danger being bullied at their school. Laura said, "Sam, I'm so glad we enrolled TO and Sammy Jr. in the self-help karate program. It's really built their self-esteem; also, living on this street has helped a lot."

"Yeah, you're right, you were jumping on my last nerve complaining about how the boys were being mistreated on the bus and at school," exclaimed Sparky.

Rocky's was usually jumping on Wednesdays and Fridays when the Alley Ratts played ball. The Ratt Pack was huddled in the far corner at a big round table where they had their pack meetings. There was Jon, Judge, Sparky, Shank, Blade, and Hoy Lee Chong.

You are probably asking yourself right now how an Oriental man got on the softball team, and more especially, how he got in the Ratt Pack. Hoy Lee Chong Grant lived on Liberty Lane with his Chinese mom and his muscular father who was ex-marine and bad to the bone. The kids on the street would refer to him as, "Mr. Grant, sir!"

Joe "Blade" Cipra asked, "Hey, Jon, we were wondering about that baby you and Cathy have cooking. When's she going to drop that squealer?"

"Another month," answered Jon. "I certainly hope that it will be a girl, you know me, and I don't want any soldiers. Not with the way our American military is heading, with what I would call, a small defense budget. You know that our government is interested in nothing but oil."

"What happens if it is a boy? Do you have a name picked out?" asked Shank.

"Well, if it's a girl, her name will be Sahara Lola, but if it's a boy, I'm calling him Zeppy Riley."

"I sure hope that boy learns how to fight, he'll need to with a name like that. Are you crazy?" yelled Judge, twirling his finger on his ear.

"God, were you born without a brain?" asked Sparky, shaking his head.

"Don't worry," said Jon without a doubt. "It'll be a girl because that is what Cathy wants."

CHAPTER 2

Thurston J. Beltow III was relaxing with a light beer and enjoying the view from the Clubhouse of the Olympia Golf and Yacht Club located in Stockton, Pennsylvania. The music in the background was Frank Sinatra singing "I've got the World on a String."

Thurston worked as vice president of the Stockton Nuclear Power Plant located in Stockton about one hundred and forty miles north of Pittsburgh, Pennsylvania, on Lake Erie. He has held many positions at the plant as engineer, general supervisor of engineering and planning, manager of engineering and planning, and now vice president. Golf has been a big part of Thurston's life, both at work and at leisure. Always on his mind are his lovely wife, Judith, and Catherine "Cathy" Michelle, Erica "Pinka" Anne, Victoria "Vicky" Erin, his three beautiful daughters. Catherine, their oldest, and her husband, Jon, were happily married and were expecting what everyone thought was going to be a girl, because Jon didn't want a soldier, naturally.

Thurston was waiting for his wife Judy to show up from her job at the Stockton Medical Center. She had been working at the medical center for thirty years as a nurse and supervisor in the nursery. Today, they are taking their daughter Catherine to get a sonogram of the baby at the hospital. As Judith enters the clubhouse at the Olympia Golf Club, she sees Thurston on the outside patio drinking a beer.

"Hi, Thurston," Judith said. "How many of those have you had? Do you remember where we're going this afternoon?"

"Yeah, of course, you think I was born yesterday, I was born at night, but not last night," barked Thurston with a grin.

"Stop it," said Judy. "You know that aggravates me!"

"I'm new, but I'm not brand new, I was born on a weekend, but not last weekend," he said, with one of his nasty little chuckles.

"Put a lid on that, let's go!" as she gave him an evil look.

"Life is good, it's good to be the king, by the way, who died and made you the boss?" asked Thurston, being a pain in the butt.

"Did you fall on your head when you were young, or were you just born stupid? Let's go."

They returned to the car and went across town to Liberty Lane to pick up Catherine.

"I'm not sure whether I want to find out the gender or not, Mom," said Cathy. "You know how Jon feels about having a boy."

"Not to worry, we know it's a girl. Women always know."

"But I hate not knowing."

"Oh well, what will be, will be," remarked Thurston. "Let's go. What time are we supposed to be there?"

"One o'clock," said Judy.

Going on the four lanes toward the hospital, Thurston says, "Oh, God, look at the traffic up ahead, there must have been a wreck."

The traffic signs were blinking and saying about the long delay, "Try to find an alternate route." There is a huge wreck at the Adam's Street exit.

"Can we take Route 90 that goes past the power plant?" asked Judy.

"Good thinking," said Thurston, heading toward the exit.

"I'm hoping it's a sweet little girl," said Cathy, biting her lip.

"Relax, Cathy, we'll be their pretty quick."

They switched over to Route 90, but while driving close to the power plant, Thurston said as he pointed, "What the hell! Those blue lights are blinking over those reactors and smoke. That says trouble."

"What?" said Judy as she swirled to look where he was pointing?

"Huh? What's happening?" asked Cathy, looking worried.

CHAPTER 3

Richard "Shank" Harmin was pipefitter foreman at the power plant and was constantly concerned about the welds. One bad weld could cause big trouble.

"There have been thirty-three serious incidents and accidents since the first recorded one, in 1952, at Chalk River in Ontario, Canada," said Shank. "I'm worried about a meltdown, like the one at Chernobyl in 1986 or the Three-Mile Island incident."

"We have the best welders in the world at this plant," Blade stated, waving his hand at Shank. Blade was a professional certified welder at the plant—the best. Joe "Blade" Cipra was a proud man of Italian descent.

"Why the hell would you call him Zeppy Riley?" asked Shank, questioning Jon with a puzzled look.

"Well," Jon said. "My grandfather's name was Giuseppe. Catherine's family all fall in the lines of English, Scotch, or Irish. The combination of the two is Zeppy for Giuseppe, and Riley for the British and the Irish. Catherine's sister Vicky has an Irish middle name of Erin, and my father-in-law, Thurston, his mom and dad were of English descent. My mom is Italian. In the future, he will probably get 'Rie' or 'Rie Guy,' get it?"

"Sometimes when you put the small pieces of the puzzle together, you can see the big picture, Jon," said Judge. "Zeppy Riley makes a whole lot of sense now. Guy is a short name for Giuseppe. I'm getting it."

Judge was a very intelligent, high IQ person of good size, six-foot-two, and husky. Judge always had something clever to say and could keep everyone amazed and laughing. His father, Judge Jock William Clydesdale II, who sits on the Supreme Court and who was very attractive to women, had a huge sense of humor. Justice Jock always kept up with the child support and the college tuitions and total support of his ex-wife, but not much loving or embracing attention to his only son Jock III. Jock III was a human resource manager for a small coating company about twelve miles west of Stockton, in the small city of Fallsburgh.

"Start spreading the news," said Sparky. "Enough said, if it's a boy, we got a Zeppy Riley, and it's catchy."

Samuel "Sparky" Simcox was a lesser man in size, but he could carry a tune. His two favorite singers were Frank Sinatra and Bob Dylan, and their songs would show up in all conversations or discussions at the pack meetings. Sparky would constantly say, "If you don't dig me, you got a hole in your soul." Sparky was the safety man at the power plant, and an emergency medical technician for the local ambulance squad.

"New sesame bread has velly fine flavor," said Hoy Lee Chong.

"Who rattled his chain?" asked Blade, slapping his head.

"Who in the hell are you talking to, Hoy Lee Chong?" asked Shank.

"I'm going to kick his ass," said Sparky, grabbing Hoy Lee Chong.

"Ooh, Sparky, 'tis like the leaf that fall from a tree into the stream, grasshopper, you in for a long journey!" said Hoy Lee Chong, in broken Chinese.

Sparky says in his best Robert De Niro New York impersonation, "You talking to me, are you talking to me, I'm standing here, I'm standing here, and it's your move."

"Knock it off, you two. Sparky, leave him alone, he could probably kick your ass," said Judge. "We have more important things to talk about."

"What about it, Jon?" asked Blade. "Is everything going according to plan?"

Jon was a weight lifter on Sundays, Mondays, and Tuesday. His muscular body would shine when he would remove his shirt. Jon took no crap from anyone, and he dared someone to say something smart to him. Jon could out talk or out cuss anyone.

"Tomorrow is the fourth of July. We will all be called to the plant tonight, but just remember two things, you don't ever—ever, I repeat—ever rat on a friend, and you keep your mouth shut," said Jon, quoting Robert De Niro.

CHAPTER 4

"What's up, Thurston?" asked Judy with fear in her eyes.

"I've got to call John Howard immediately," said Thurston. "We can't go to the hospital right now." Thurston dialed, and John answered right away.

"What's up with the blue lights, John? Is their something wrong with the reactors?" he asked, coughing and clearing his throat.

John Howard was the general manager in charge of the afternoon shift at the plant. John was very meticulous about anything that could happen at the plant. He had two degrees from the Nuclear Science and Engineering Institute, BS, MS, Missouri University, St. Louis, Missouri.

"We have a situation here, it's looking like the roof fell in on the number one nuclear reactor." explained John, looking for some support from Thurston.

"God," said Thurston. "You have to get water on it right away. You know what to do. Did you turn on the pumps that are connected to the lake? I hope none of the nuclear fuel rods are melting down."

"What about my sonogram?" asked Catherine with tears in her eyes.

"That's the last thing on my mind right now, Cathy," said Thurston. "Judy, take the car, swing by the club and pick up my car, Cathy can drive, and go home until you hear from me. I'm thinking the hospital is going to be busy for a while, if we have a meltdown."

"John, you still there?" asked Thurston. "I'm going to set up the security to keep everyone out of the area, and you sound the alarm for all nontechnical employees to evacuate the plant. Also, I need to call the International Atomic Energy Authority and Albert, the CEO, to put them on alert. I will also alert the National Guard and the local authorities. We don't want a panic in the city."

Thurston would get hold of Jon Van Lorne, his son-in-law, Shank Harmin, Sparky Simcox, Blade Cipra, and Hoy Lee Chong Grant, who knows the entire system. He would also get hold of Judge Clydesdale III as a consultant, who knows more about nuclear power than anyone working there, to somehow keep things straight. Please let those idiots be sober.

Thurston called John Howard back to get a report. "My God," said John, "I never dreamed anything like this could happen at our plant, we watch and record the readings on the gauges constantly. The engineers and technicians report to me every half hour to watch for any malfunction. They physically check each reactor to see if the nuclear fuel rods are clear. It almost looks like some one has intentionally tampered with the fuel rods. I have no explanation."

"Thank God we're getting all the cleaning personnel out of there," said Thurston, wiping sweat. "I called all the heads of the maintenance and security. We have to hold the maintenance and technical people working on your shift over. We need to identify the problem and attack it as soon as possible. Are we keeping the reactor watered down?"

"Yes," said John. "We are pouring a huge number of gallons per minute. That should keep it cool. What we have to be careful of is an explosion, which would separate the fuel rods, and God help us if that happens, because it would be total exposure to radiation. Wait, we are getting a huge hissing sound out of the no. 1 reactor right now. Oh my God, get out!"

"What the hell is going on, John?" said Thurston in panic.

"Get out of the building now, Thurston, get out!"

CHAPTER 5

Catherine Michelle Beltow graduated from West Virginia University in 1997 with a degree in forestry. She and Jonathon Van Lorne had been dating and cared a lot about each other since her sophomore year at the university. Jon was working as a security guard at the Stockton Power Plant almost two years, and he and Catherine had planned a private destination wedding on the islands just off the shores of Port Clinton, Ohio. The islands were named Put-in-Bay, Large Bass, Middle Bass, and Little Bass Islands. They set off on a three-hour tour, which ended on one of the islands that had a winery. They met a wonderful couple, the Howells, who were one of the couples on the tour. The Howells said that they go on these mini-tours all the time, and that they would witness Jon and Catherine's wedding. Cathy liked Mr. Howell because he had the same name as her father, Thurston III. Jon and Cathy were married in front of an adjacent lighthouse by the operator of the boat who was also an ordained minister, Captain William Gilligan. They stayed overnight at a bed-and-breakfast on Put-in-

Bay. They returned on a ferry boat to Port Clinton in the afternoon the next day. They spent the remainder of the day at Cedar Point Amusement Park. Judith Beltow had a small party and would plan a later reception for them at their home at Highland Drive on Carlin Heights. Jon had previously purchased a home on the end of Liberty Lane, which had no outlet.

Catherine was in the process of purchasing and wanting to operate a discount greenhouse. She would grow plants from seeds and sell them to the larger greenhouse dealers. The greenhouse had everything you would need to make all of this happen. Thurston's younger brother, Levi, painted a huge sign to display in the front.

Jon was constantly bugged by the fact that he worked at a nuclear power plant, which produced steam by nuclear fission to turn the turbines and produce electrical energy by powering the generators. He would rather use the plutonium for military strength. His thoughts were that we could not withstand another conflict like Operation Desert Storm. Not with the depleted military. Operation Desert Storm was to deter any invasion of Kuwait's oil-rich neighbors, Saudi Arabia, and called for an immediate, complete, and unconditional withdrawal of all Iraqi forces from Kuwait. It stipulated that if Iraqi dictator Saddam Hussein did not remove his troops from Kuwait, the US-led coalition would drive them out, and they did.

On February 27, 1991, Kuwait City was liberated. The president called for a cease fire and ended the war.

Desert Storm had raised questions as to what lessons China and other nations had drawn from the US military engagements in the Middle East and Balkans.

On Friday, February 26, 1993, Middle Eastern terrorism had arrived on American soil—with a bang! The World Trade Center bombing occurred when a truck bomb was detonated below the north tower of the World Trade Center in New York, NY. The urea nitrate-hydrogen gas enhanced device was intended to knock the north tower into the south tower, bringing both towers down and killing thousands of people. It failed to do so but did kill six people and injured more than a thousand. In 1994, four conspirators were convicted of carrying out the bombings. In November 1997, two more were convicted: Ramzi Yousef, the mastermind, and Eyad Ismoil, who drove the truck carrying the bomb.

American interest and intervention in the Balkans is peripheral. Europe needed to take over to bring peace and stability to Southeastern Europe. American combat troops needed to withdraw now that the crisis has passed in Bosnia and Kosovo.

"Our US government officials need to wake up and pay attention," Jon would say.

CHAPTER 6

"All right." said Jon. "We are going over this one more time. Judge and I have spent a lot of time on this, and we've done a ton of research."

Sparky was singing one of Bob Dylan's songs to Hoy Lee Chong. "That song is for you, Chong, alone and without a home," spouted Sparky, rubbing his eyes as if he was crying.

"Stop it!" shouted Judge. "Tomorrow is the day it's all happening. We have to get it straight, you little worm."

"Bob Dylan received many awards for his endless music," said Sparky.

"Tell that to someone who cares. Now listen up!" said Jon. "Judge and I have done all the pre-work to cause a partial meltdown at the plant. It has happened naturally at other plants so we know that it's safe. It will appear as if no. 1 reactor's roof has fallen, and we are jamming one of the nuclear fuel rods to cause cooling system malfunction. No damage, only fuel integrity. No release of radiation. The reactor will only give symptoms of roof failure, a lot of steam. They will put tons of water on it to cool and keep it from potentially exploding. It will be set on a timer to partially block one of the nuclear fuel rods with graphite debris, and in twenty-four hours or less, it will be completely clear. This diversion will give us time for what we are attempting to do. All of us will be called back to work at the plant today as soon as my father-in-law, Thurston, gets wind of it. We will appear at work as if we are startled and ready to help. We will stay throughout the night setting up security and being prepared for whatever comes up."

"Whoa, that's Cathy calling. I got to answer this. Hello…," answered Jon.

"Jon, oh my God, something is happening at the plant. My father is there with John Howard, and I think it's something serious. Mom and I didn't make it to the hospital for the sonogram. He said to stay here until we heard from him. What should we do?" asked Cathy, trying not to get upset.

"Just stay there, I'll call as soon as I know something. All of the pack will have to be there. We'll leave as soon as your dad calls with orders. Bye."

"Shank, what about the trucks?" asked Jon with his arms stretched out.

"No problem, Blade and I have access any time we need them," said Shank, who had some leverage at the Pennsylvania Army National Guard.

Thurston Beltow III had been affiliated with the Pennsylvania Army National Guard, located at an armory about ten miles west of Stockton since 1964. Thurston had acquired his engineering degree from the Department of Nuclear Science and Education at MIT (Massachusetts

Institute of Technology) in Cambridge, Massachusetts, which provided the opportunity for graduate students interested in advancing the frontier of nuclear science and engineering. He attended OCS (Officers Training School) at the National Guard Unit and became a second lieutenant, promoted to first lieutenant, later to captain, and then colonel. He was made company commander of the unit. Some of the Ratt Pack enlisted in the National Guard Unit in 1995. Shank, Blade, Sparky, and Hoy Lee Chong signed up. Shank had been promoted over the years to staff sergeant in charge of all the equipment in the motor pool. The unit was a transportation, construction unit that had heavy equipment and trucks and plenty of construction tools. The construction unit continued working on projects about forty-five miles southeast of Stockton. Thurston, being in charge of the unit had no idea what his son-in-law was doing. They spent their two-week summer camp there and also did bivouac on weekends there. (Means they stayed in tents overnight). They were putting together portable bridges that spanned small rivers. Blade was a Specialist 5, a truck driver for the unit. Sparky and Hoy Lee Chong were corporals. Hoy Lee Chong was a construction instrument man who operated the survey instruments needed for the projects. The unit was then working on a project of installing a bridge across a waterway that the rolling vehicles couldn't cross. They would install a bridge across any span in less than twenty four hours and would withstand the weight of the heavy-duty rolling vehicles, including tanks. Shank and Blade were observing the area and found a perfect spot to hide the two modules that they will be pulling out of the power plant. It was a huge cavern, which could be shielded with dirt, using National Guard equipment. Shank and Blade said they could supply two-tractor trailer rigs when needed at the nuclear power plant.

"I'm going to smack the hell out of this Hoy Lee Chong if he doesn't stop that," said Sparky. "He speaks perfect English, and he keeps it up with this broken Chinese crap."

Hoy Lee Chong Grant was a total genius who had graduated early (three years) from MIT with a degree in nuclear science and engineering. He at times knew much more than the professors. His grandfather, J. Walker Grant, was one of the original people attending the groundbreaking of Stockton's nuclear power plant, who worked there for twenty years. Hoy Lee Chong grew up knowing everything to know about nuclear power systems.

"Bite me, Sparky," said Hoy Lee Chong in very plain English.

"Now," said Jon, "as I said before, we will stay throughout the night and make our move in the morning. The plant will be clear except for a few needed technicians, adequate security, safety people, craft supervision and crafts, the four of us, Sparky, Shank, Blade, and me. Of course, Hoy Lee Chong and Judge will keep my father-in-law and all the technicians busy. Most of the people in Stockton will not be alerted to the incident, so they will carry on their picnics, cookouts, and fireworks for the Fourth of July."

"Shank and Blade," said Judge. "You will wear the protective clothing that we have acquired this year for two reasons. One, as a safety measure, and two, we will appear to be working. No one will question anything. No one will recognize you. Naturally, Shank, you and Blade will leave the plant and return at seven o'clock in the morning with the rigs and pass safely through the gates. You will move straight to number two warehouse, which is protected by two sets of security gates, which Jon will let you though before you come to what they call the Bunker. There will be armed guards at the Bunker, so act like you know what you're doing. Jon will get you access, and lo and behold, there will be the two sealed modular trailers. They are sealed and protected by the government so that no one can trace them. You will hook up and drag them out. This will happen so fast no one will know what happened. All the gates will be relocked. Security won't pay any attention because you are in military vehicles, and they have seen similar movements before."

"Here's Thurston," said Jon. "Hello, Jon here."

"God, I hope you birds haven't been drinking too much. We have an incident at the plant, and I'm hoping and praying that it's not going to turn into an accident. All the gauges are showing big trouble on no. 1 reactor. Is everyone there, Judge, Shank…

"We're all here, we'll be there as quickly as possible, Thurston," replied Jon.

"Okay, Ratts, load up in your own cars, I'll meet you at the plant. Don't forget your badges to get through the gate," said Jon.

CHAPTER 7

"I'm calling Vicky and Pinka, Mom," said Cathy. "Hello, Pinka, I can't believe we didn't get to the hospital for that sonogram. Something happened at the power plant, and Mom and I are at my house waiting to hear. Dad or Jon are supposed to call us as soon as they know what happened. How's Bernice? Is she still up and running?"

"Yeah, Bernice is still perking," said Pinka. "What's going on? Is there going to be a meltdown? You know that always scared me. That's why I'm never coming back to that radioactive city, Stockton. You and Jon need to get your dumb asses the hell out of there."

"Give me some room. The greenhouse isn't costing as much money now. Some day I might even make a profit, but not in the near future," said Cathy, brushing a fly away from her face.

"That's what I mean. You and Jon are spinning your wheels. You have a good education, graduated the top of your class, go and get yourself a real job. What happened with those jobs you were applying for in Florida?" asked Pinka.

"They have called me for interviews, but I just don't have the nerve yet. Some day I'm taking them up on it and move to Florida, whether Jon wants to come or not," said Cathy, shrugging her shoulders. "What's happening with you? Got you a man yet?"

"Yes, he works construction and takes classes at the university. You know me, I'm a sucker, and I fall in love with all the good-looking, not so rich ones. Anyway, his name is Michael Trainer, and he is a Morgantown hunk," said Pinka; she was hoping to hook this one.

"Okay, good luck with that hunk. I'm calling Vicky to let her know what's happening."

"Bye," replied Pinka, thinking of her handsome hunk.

"You all right, mom?" asked Cathy. "Get yourself a glass of wine or something to drink. It may be a while before they call, I'm calling Vicky."

Victoria Erin Beltow had graduated from Marshall University, located in Huntington, West Virginia, as an elementary teacher, and later, received a master's degree from West Virginia University. She applied, interviewed, and was working as a reading specialist, in Prince William School District at Belmont Elementary School, in Woodbridge, Virginia.

"Hey, Vicky, this is Cathy, what's happening? I wanted to tell you that I didn't get to the hospital for the sonogram, so we still don't know the gender. Mom keeps telling me it's a girl, and you know Jon, he doesn't want a soldier. How's the job? Oh, by the way, there's something going on at the power plant, maybe serious. Mom and I might be down to see Pinka if we have to evacuate. I want as far away from here as possible."

"Job's good, I love it. I'm in a real nice apartment complex, a lot of shopping outlets. That's terrible about that freaking power plant. I keep telling you to get out of Stockton. That place is a constant worry. I'll never go back there."

"I know, but Jon thinks we are pretty well established and doesn't want to leave. I would leave in a minute. I just want to get this baby born."

"Yeah," yelled Vicky. "How long you been pregnant anyhow? It seems like forever. Will you come on? Is mom okay?"

"Yeah, I'm making her drink wine to settle her down. Dad keeps her on edge all the time, with that constant talking that he does."

"He's a flapper all right, but we still love him," exclaimed Vicky.

"Okay, got to go. I'll call you later, bye!" said Cathy, closing her cell phone.

"Bye," said Vicky.

CHAPTER 8

Jon and the Ratt Pack all arrived at the power plant about the same time. They showed their badges and went through the metal detector as fast as possible. Thurston met them and told them that John Howard was upset and that they shouldn't be in the plant. He got John back on the radio and asked what the hell was going on. John responded and said apologetically, "I'm sorry, Thurston. We thought the place was going to blow up. Here all the hissing and whooshing was the water trying to get through the thirty-six-inch pipe back to the lake, we're under control now. It will take us all night to figure out what happened. I believe everything is going to be all right. The gauges showed a rod failure combined with a few operating errors. The fuel channels must have cleared themselves because they are unclogged and restored. We have to inspect the fuel rods for damage and make sure everything is clear. Also, the roof is secure."

"That's great news! We will all have to stick around tonight until we get the all clear, which won't be until late tomorrow. Plan on spending the night, Jon," said Thurston, lighting a cigarette and pacing as he spoke.

"I'll call Cathy and Judy and let them know we're all right and that the worst is over," said Jon.

"Cathy," said Jon, "not to worry, it's over. We had quite a scare, but everything is under control. We will have to keep an eye on things to make sure there is no reoccurrence. We should be able to leave by late morning. Tell your mom she can come and pick up Thurston. There is no reason for him to stay."

"Oh my God, this baby is kicking like crazy. I'm scheduling another sonogram the day after tomorrow. It's the fourth tomorrow, you know. Are you sure we want to know the baby's gender?" asked Cathy uncomfortably.

"Yeah, right now I do because I'm not sure what is going to happen from this point on," replied Jon, shrugging apologetically.

"That's crazy, Jon, what you and your gang are doing. I know it is in your heart to do it, but it's so dangerous. I want this baby to have a father, you know," Cathy pleaded.

"It will be over before you know it. Once we have the modules, there will be no contact between us. I love you, bye," answered Jon.

"Bye," said Cathy.

"Everything is working perfectly," Jon told the pack. "I believe we are going to pull this off."

"Life isn't about how to survive the storm, but how to dance in the rain," said Hoy Lee Chong, who was quoting a famous saying.

"What kind of crap is that, Chong?" asked Sparky. "If brains were dynamite, you wouldn't have enough to blow the hairs off a flea's ass."

"You know Amish, Sparky boy," said Hoy Lee Chong. "Go screweth thyself."

"I'm going to knock both of you assholes out," said Blade. "What time should Shank and I leave to pick up the trucks, Judge?"

"I'm thinking around five o'clock am, which should get you to the armory and back in plenty of time," said Judge, pointing at his watch. "Jon is in charge of security, so there should be no problem."

"Didn't Frank Sinatra sing something about facing the final curtain?" yelled Sparky, completely assured that everything was going good.

"Is there a knob to turn that egghead, Sparky, off?" shouted Shank. "He is jumping on my last nerve. I'm going to rip that boy's head off."

"Cool it, guys," said Jon. "We got a long night ahead of us."

At seven o'clock in the morning, two truck cabs were pulling up to the front gates of the power plant. Jon had already alerted the guards that the drivers have government papers to get through.

"Let them in because they have to make a pick up at the number two warehouse," Jon told the guards.

Jon and Sparky let them through the two sets of gates as they approached the two armed guards who flagged them down and told them they couldn't go any further.

"It's all right," Jon approached the guards. "They have papers from the government to pick up the two modules that are inside the Bunker."

"I got your papers swinging. We have strict orders that no one gets near this Bunker, and it's our job to stop them if they try. Why do those drivers have protective clothing on, and you have no jurisdiction over those modules. If you try anything, it is our job to stop you, understand? We don't know who you are. You could be terrorists. We answer to no one but the governor."

Wow, Jon wasn't expecting this. The whole plan has gone to hell in a basket, and there is hardly anything that he could do.

"Listen, guys, I'm not trying to give you a hard time, but if you look at those papers, they are signed by the president," said Jon.

"Christ, why didn't you tell us that? Okay, we'll give you all the help you need," the guards responded.

The doors of the Bunker swung open, and the trucks pulled in as fast as possible.

"Hook up as fast as you can, we have to get these modules out of here," Jon yelled. "Take them directly to the location that's designated on the orders."

Jon went closer to the rig and told Shank, "Back the modules into the caverns and cover the entrance with dirt. Its forty miles, so be careful."

Jon told the armed guards that they could leave because there was nothing left to watch. The trucks passed back through the front gates at seven forty five o'clock. Jon and Sparky relocked all of the gates.

"God, I thought we were dusters when those armed guards wouldn't let us in the Bunker." said Sparky. "Were those papers really signed by the president?"

"No," said Jon. "Fortunately, they didn't even look at them, but I had to take that chance."

CHAPTER 9

"Sum-bitch, Thurston, the freaking modules are gone," said Albert Fu Fu, the CEO of the power plant. "I left you in charge while I was in Japan and Korea this last month. What the hell happened? Were you asleep or what? I warned you about terrorists. Those terrorists have unbelievable, sneaky ways to enter the plant. They have no fear of ending their lives on a mission. They can make up papers to get in the gate. They can steal army vehicles by force. How did they get past the armed guards? Those armed guards are taught, shoot to kill. Why did your son-in-law allow this to happen? I hope Jon, or you, aren't involved in this. You are aware of what is in those modules, aren't you?"

"Yes, I'm aware," said Thurston. "I haven't been able to get in touch with Jon or Jock Clydesdale. My fear is that this may have been an inside job. Someone had to let all these things happen. I truly fear that Jon and Jock are involved."

"You better tell that jackass son-in-law of yours that he is going to jail if he doesn't get those modules back here, and I mean now," said Albert. "This isn't a joke. We are talking big prison time if he continues to hold those modules. Those two can't be that dumb."

Jon and Judge were staying in an apartment in Pittsburgh, Pennsylvania, owned by Judge's former classmate at MIT in Cambridge, Clayton Buffett, who was a newscaster for WTAE, channel 4, in Pittsburgh. He and Judge started at MIT, majoring in nuclear science and engineering but ended up graduating together in social science at Pitt. Clayton has agreed to be the letter carrier for Jon and Jock. The letter will be addressed to the governor of Pennsylvania and to the president. Clayton understood what these two were trying to accomplish and how they feel about the weak military, but also knew that he was aiding and abetting two jug heads. He is well aware that there is a crime here. He could go to jail.

That evening, Clayton was questioning Jon and Jock about what they were doing. "Why is this so important? You could get yourselves killed messing with the government like this."

Judge, being the philosopher that he was, said to Clayton, "We studied English in college, and do you remember Robert Burns, the poet."

"Of course," said Clayton.

"He wrote something about seeing ourselves as other people see us. We don't want other nations to see the United States as killing mongrels because of their overabundance of nuclear weapons. Do you know why there's a Noble Peace Prize?"

Clayton stared at him, wandering what in the hell that had to do with their now ridiculous conversation.

"It's an interesting story, and it is relevant. Alfred Nobel was the inventor of dynamite. You know that. It was definitely a useful tool for clearing land, mining, and building railroads, etc. But it was also used on the battlefield. Many people were killed because of dynamite. In 1888, Nobel's brother Emil died, I can't remember where. Many newspapers got the story mixed up and mistook the brother for Alfred and ran huge, flashing headlines, 'The merchant of death is dead.' It went on to say that Alfred Nobel became wealthy by finding ways to injure and kill people faster then ever. Nobel was so shook up by what he read about himself, he decided to change his legacy. He left his entire fortune to the establishment of the Nobel Peace Prize. I read that somewhere."

Jon said, "It's like a controlled substance dealer feeling so bad about destroying people's lives that he leaves his money to establish many drug rehabilitation clinics. Actually, we don't want the world to look at the United States as 'Merchants of Death' with our nuclear arms. We just want their respect and not think of us as that weak, vulnerable target that we have made ourselves. I got a text message from Cathy today that we are going to have a boy. I want him to grow up in a nation that is safe and has no fear."

"Hey," said Judge. "We are going to have ourselves a Zeppy Riley! Congratulations, Jon."

"How soon will you have the letter ready?" asked Clayton.

"They're ready now," said Jon. "There is one addressed to the governor and one addressed to the president. We want to deliver them to the governor's office early tomorrow morning. These have to be in their hands as soon as possible."

Jon and Judge could not have found a better person to carry their letter to the governor. Clayton was very popular and could be, in the future, a possible candidate for governor himself.

Jon asked Judge before they were going to bed, "Do you think we have everything covered in the letter?"

"I hope so," said Judge. "Yeah, I really hope so," he prayed.

CHAPTER 10

Clayton was up early and drove to the governor's office and arrived at ten o'clock. He approached the secretary right away and asked to speak to the governor; it was urgent.

"Everyone who comes in here has an urgent reason to see him," responded the secretary. "What is this concerning?"

"I am a newscaster from a well-known station in Pittsburgh. I am here to deliver two important letters to the governor and to the president. It is concerning the two modules that were removed from the Stockton, Pennsylvania, Nuclear Power Plant. They were taken yesterday, and he is probably expecting me. I have information as to who is holding them."

"My God, yes, I will alert him right away that you are here, one moment, please." muttered the secretary, running to tell the governor.

The governor appeared from out of his office and said, "I hope you people know what you are doing. This is a very dangerous, absolute crazy game that you are playing. This is critical."

"Governor, don't kill the messenger. I am Clayton Buffett from channel 4 news. I am only here to deliver letters to let you know what is on the playing table between the president and yourself and the perpetrators holding the modules, nothing more. The letters were left at my office. They were addressed to you and the president. I felt it was my obligation to deliver them because of an accompanying note saying what had happened and that they needed my help and trusted me. They said the letters will explain everything. These people need to be treated with respect. They may have done something out of line, but they feel that they did it for what they think is a good purpose. You may not agree, but they want to negotiate."

"All I know right now is that there are some really upset people at the power plant, and that whoever is responsible, they are calling them terrorists. That means that there is no mercy. They want them eliminated right away with military force," said the governor, not making things easy.

"These people who are holding the modules want a peaceful agreement, and the modules will be returned safe and unharmed. Please take the letters, read them, make a decision, and respond. I have no idea where to find them, but they left me a number where they can be reached with your response, and they will turn themselves in to the local authorities."

"Well, Mr. Buffett, we are holding you until I can contact the president to see what direction he wants to go with this. I'm hoping that you are not aiding and abetting these people because it could mean trouble for you. Right now, I trust you because you seem to be a sincere person. I will release you as soon as the president says it is all right."

"Governor, I want you to fax me that letter that is addressed to me," said the president. "From what you are telling me, these people don't seem like radicals. Let's read the letters before we decide what to do."

The two letters were identical, one to the governor and the other to the president. They read:

Mr. President,

> My name is Jonathon Van Lorne. Jock Clydesdale and I have in our possession (2) modules that were heavily guarded at the nuclear power plant in Stockton, Pennsylvania. The modules are safe, cannot be traced, and can be returned at any time. We are not trying to create an issue of fear. We are not planning any negotiations to sell or to give the modules to anyone. Our mission is to bring strength and credibility back to the United States military and the national security. Congress is spending less on the military each year. Our defense budget is smaller then it was fifteen years ago. To put it bluntly, the appalling statistics prove just how thoroughly the current administration has depleted our military. The United States of America is becoming a weak, easy target. Twenty-six years ago, there were two world supreme powers that got respect…no more…
>
>   Over a twenty-year period, we have allowed China to swipe over 60 percent of our nuclear secrets. We blame the CIA for all that

Chinese thievery. You expect us to be ready for war with Korea, the Middle East, and now Southeastern Europe, yet our defense budget keeps depleting. The situation is extremely crucial. We have videos of the world's current madmen in Korea, Iraq, Egypt, and Iran watching their military parades. There's China, with their unprecedented military buildup. The Chinese generals standing attentively at their military functions, watching their massive machinery roll by. China wants to take over Taiwan as they watch their thousands of Chinese soldiers march in perfect step. North Korea wants South Korea, and their tanks will roll right through the DMZ, which is all that separates them. There is no telling what Iran would do with nuclear weapons. They have the knowledge and technology; eventually they will have the bomb! A lot of this Jock and I have read or heard, naturally.

I, Jon Van Lorne, have an unborn son coming in early August. Do I feel that the world is a safer place? Absolutely not…

What are we laying on the bargaining table? All we ask in return for the modules we are holding. Number one, we expect the government officials and Congress to take a good look at the defense spending. We are low on soldiers, tanks, missiles, planes, and carriers. We are not at a layback, peaceful condition and the United States generals have made their statements about the downfall of the military. Number two, we would like to see the military budget doubled or tripled. Not an easy task.

Number three, we would like an unconditional pardon for all the people who were part of this endeavor, knowing that we were all vulnerable for punishment. But in our hearts we knew there was a message to be delivered to save the sagging United States of America and bring back our strength.

Thank you. We will wait for your response.

CHAPTER 11

"Governor, these jobs don't get any easier, do they?" said the president after reading the letter. "These people are absolutely correct in what they are saying, but they have definitely broken the law. This crime is punishable by law in the umpteenth degree. First, I can't see any of them maintaining their jobs at the power plant, including that vice president Thurston Beltow. He is due for retirement anyway. I don't believe they can even stay in the state of Pennsylvania, and I don't know how much strength and unconditional power that I have to keep them from prosecution. It is certainly heart warming that people would love their country so much that they would put themselves out on a limb like that. I understand that the modules can be recovered without incident, but how do we keep the CEO, Albert Fu Fu out of this. He wants to deal with them as terrorists, a conspiracy. Do you have any suggestions, Governor?"

"I let that newscaster, Clayton Buffett that brought the letters, off the hook. I can't believe he had anything to do with this, too honest and sincere. My suggestion is this. These people got our attention. Actually, they just had a bad choice of how to do it. They meant no harm. Everything can be brought back to normal in a day. There is a huge bonding between these six characters. They work together and play together. They all live on the same street. They are known as the Ratt Pack. They have a softball team called Rocky's Alley Ratts. They all work at the power plant. They are very close. Jon Van Lorne and Jock Clydesdale seem to be the leaders of the group. My suggestion is a separation of all, and not one of them can keep residence in Pennsylvania. Jock and Hoy Lee Chong Grant are geniuses in nuclear power and the fission processes that go with nuclear power for heat and electricity and the making of nuclear weapons. We have a contact in Chicago, Illinois, Jude Yamin, who can get them into the nuclear science laboratories located in Chicago. Richard Harmin and Joseph Cipra, with our help, can get into the pipefitting and welding unions and not miss a day of work. Jon will be the night manager for the Hampton Inn in Wheeling, West Virginia. Samuel Simcox will be working at Weirton Steel Corporation as a safety director. Thurston Beltow will take a retirement from the power plant and find residence and work, in West Virginia, where his parents live. Jon and Jock will have to spend at least fifteen days in the unguarded facility in Philadelphia, Pennsylvania, and pay a $20,000 fine, each. This will appease the CEO, Albert Fu Fu, at the power plant. We will purchase and resale all their homes on Liberty Lane. You have the power to pardon these people."

"I agree with everything you said," replied the president, "I will make a sincere promise to all of those involved that we are taking it seriously and hope that we can bring back the credibility that the United States of America has been lacking."

"All right," said the governor, hoping he wouldn't lose his job. Deep down he knew he wouldn't.

"I am setting up a hearing with the honorable Justice Jock William Clydesdale, presiding and witnessing, which I have the authority to call up the six people involved with this action and give them my total and final response. It will be presented and set up exactly like you said, Governor, and if they do not except those terms, they will be tried and punished by the full extent of the law, for conspiracy and terrorism."

Needless to say, everyone accepted the terms from the hearing, so everyone was saying their good-byes, because everyone was going to a different destination. Jon and Jock would serve their sentences and keep a long-time relationship, being sent to the same correctional institute.

"I've rented an apartment in Wheeling, Jon," said Catherine. "The Hampton Inn seems like a pretty nice place to work. I think you'll like it. My cousin, Joseph Caironich, who lives in Jefferson, Ohio, may be able to get you a job in Ashtabula County at an assembly factory. Otherwise, Zeppy Riley might have to grow up in Wheeling, West Virginia. I'm staying with Pinka in Morgantown, West Virginia, until you finish serving your time."

"Okay," said Jon. "This correctional institution isn't all that bad. Judge and I still see each other quit often.

The food is good, and we have all kinds of privileges. We both thank God that it didn't go in a more tragic direction. They could have hung us, you know. We'll just wait it out, and I hope our new beginning works out. I can't wait to see Zeppy Riley."

CHAPTER 12

Thurston and Judith sold their home in Stockton and purchased a home in West Virginia where they were raised. Thurston interviewed and accepted a job at Weirton Steel Corporation as general supervisor of engineering and planning. Judy landed a job as a private nurse taking care of boy (Brian) who was brain damaged at birth. Thurston and Judy's parents still lived in Weirton, which was a small steel-making city that got its name from the founder of Weirton Steel Corporation, E. T. Weir. Thurston loved the location of Weirton, which was about three miles east of Steubenville, Ohio, and thirty miles west of Pittsburgh, Pennsylvania.

"I love this view from our house, Thurston," said Judy, being pleased.

The house overlooked a beautiful tree filled setting and Pleasant Valley Country Club, where Thurston had become a member.

"Yeah," said Thurston. "It is majestic. Things have worked out well. I'll receive a full pension from the power plant and work for Weirton Steel Corporation. Sparky Simcox has also been hired as a safety director.

"That's wonderful," said Judy. "Cathy is staying with Pinka in Morgantown until Jon gets released from Philadelphia. Her sonogram shows a boy, and I'm talking Cathy into putting Riley Giuseppe on the birth certificate."

"Good," said Thurston. "You know he'll always be Zeppy Riley to them."

Thurston Had always had an interest in England because both of his parents had roots there. His Beltow name stems back in ancestry to Staffordshire County, England, beginning with John and Lucy Mary Beltow. Thurston's mom's name was Blackshaw, which also traces back to John Blackshaw of Chester, Cheshire, England. Thurston and Judy had given their three daughters queen names, Catherine, Anne, and Victoria.

"The British Isles are odd," said Judy. "Many people feel that Great Britain or the United Kingdom is England. Wrong! Actually, Great Britain is the largest island in the British Isles, which includes England, Wales, and Scotland. The United Kingdom consists of England, Wales, Scotland, and Northern Ireland. London is the capital of England. London is also the capital of the United Kingdom."

"Thank you for the history lesson," said Thurston. "You think I was born yesterday? I was born at night, but not last night."

"Will you stop? You are wearing that out. If I want any crap out of you, Thurston, I'll squeeze it out," said Judy as she was talking about England. "Guess what?

England occupies most of Great Britain and contains 84 percent of the United Kingdom population, which includes about fifty million people. There are seven million people in London."

The United Kingdom of Great Britain and Northern Ireland is situated northwest of the European continent between the Atlantic Ocean and the North Sea. The United Kingdom is a member of the European Union. The union flag is the national flag of the United Kingdom. It is British. It is called the union flag because it symbolizes the administrative union of the countries of the United Kingdom. It is made up of the individual flags of three of the kingdom's countries, which are England, of Scotland, and of Northern Ireland. Beginning in 1921, only the northern part of Ireland has been part of the United Kingdom. Wales was not a kingdom but a principality. They were not included in the union flag.

"The British government runs the United Kingdom. Naturally, the leader of the government is the prime minister. The United Kingdom is a parliamentary democracy with a constitutional monarch as head of state, that would be the queen, Thurston," continued Judy. "Parliament represents the people and elected representatives are placed in the House of Commons. Parliament is made up of three parts," spouted Judy.

"Be obscure clearly," exclaimed Thurston as he quoted E. B. White.

"The Wizard of Oz just called, he said your brain is ready, Thurston. Now, as I was saying, the queen is the official head of state, and she has the final say on whether a bill becomes law, of course, because she's a woman. The

House of Lords is made up of people who have inherited family titles. Their job is to 'double-check' new laws to make sure they will work."

"What about the members of the House of Commons. You didn't think I knew anything, they are the ones who create the bills, correct, Judy?"

"The House of Commons members are elected by local residents to represent an area of the country in Parliament, Thurston. Get it?"

"I can't believe what I am finding out about my mom's ancestors on the Internet, it is the largest family, ever," said Thurston. "I have traced ancestry to John Blackshaw of Chester, Cheshire County, England, who was born in 1505. Five generations later, in 1677. Ship Phillip, owned by crown-appointed Governor Carteret of New Jersey, listed Thomas Blackshaw as a passenger, sailing from London to New Jersey. Thomas Blackshaw was one of the first to establish family in colonial America. Along with Drake, Hands, and Hendrick, they were listed as early settlers of Piscataway, New Jersey. The Blackshaw migration spread out to the Carolinas, Pennsylvania, Virginia, and West Virginia, which descended down to my Grandfather Otha Wade Blackshaw. There is one piece of folklore, in a letter, during King Henry the VIII reign, which is very uncertain and puzzling."

There is tremendous English folklore that has developed and trickled down over a number of centuries. Some stories have been traced back to there roots, while the origin of others is uncertain and disputed. England abounds with folklore in all forms from such obvious manifestations as the traditional Robin Hood tales, the Briton-inspired Arthurian legend, the poetic tale of Beowulf, to contemporary urban legends and facets of cryptozoology such as the Beast of Bodmin Moor. English folklore is largely drawn from Germanic, Celtic, and Christian sources.

"What's that, Thurston?" asked Judy. "Why are you puzzled?"

CHAPTER 13

On July 21, 1998, Jon was turned loose after his assigned fifteen days at the Cross Corrections Center in Philadelphia, Pennsylvania. Cross Center is a minimum-security prison, commonly referred to as a camp. No walls or fences at all, about five hundred very low-risk inmates. He said his good-byes to Judge Clydesdale and was taxied to the airport for his flight to Pittsburgh. Judge was taxied in the opposite direction for his flight to Chicago. Jon would arrive at Pittsburgh International Airport at 7:00 pm.

Judy went along with Cathy to pick Jon up. They would drop Judy off in Weirton before they continued to Wheeling, West Virginia.

"Hi, Jon," said Judy as she and Cathy both gave him big hugs. "Do we need to pick up any luggage?" Jon had just gotten off of the tram, smiling.

"No," replied Jon. "All I have is this shoulder bag and this drag-along carry-on." They exited on the speed walk toward the extended parking.

"I'm so glad you are back, seems like you have been gone forever," said Cathy. "Anyway, as I told you, all our furniture has been delivered from our house in Stockton to Wheeling. You are going to love the apartment I picked out, and it's only two blocks away from the Hampton Inn. We managed to get both vehicles moved. I'm driving the Jeep."

"Well, all right, let's go," said Jon. "I'm anxious to see our new home in Wheeling, West Virginia. The Hampton Inn has me scheduled to work Monday evening. That will at least give me a couple of days to check things out. Thanks for coming with Cathy, grandma-to-be."

Wheeling is a city in Ohio County and also the county seat. Its nickname is the Friendly City and was once the capital of West Virginia. It is located in what they call the northern panhandle, across the Ohio River from the state of Ohio.

Jon started to work at the Hampton Inn on Monday. He wasn't crazy about wearing a shirt and tie, but he was the night manager. They put another manager, Phil Gates, with Jon for a few days to show him how everything operated.

"Most of the people are checked in and settled in by the time you get here, so it's mostly sorting and organizing the daily receipts, keep and post the wake-up calls, and watch that television. There may be some late check-ins, but not many. They call this the graveyard shift. The main thing is to keep yourself busy to keep from falling asleep, which you don't want to do. Upper management frowns on that. I saw on your papers that you are married. Are you from around here?" asked Phil, yawning a little.

"My wife Cathy and I just moved here from Stockton, Pennsylvania," said Jon. "She's due to have a baby in about a week."

"That's great, do you know what she's having?" asked Phil.

"Yeah," Jon said loudly. "It's going to be a boy!"

On August 1, Judy was trying to get in touch of Thurston on the golf course and not having a whole lot of luck. Jon had taken Cathy to Wheeling Hospital having labor pains.

Judy was getting angry not being able to reach Thurston. She called the Pro Shop at the golf course trying to reach him.

"I can't reach him on his phone. Could someone go out and get him?" asked Judy. "My daughter is in the hospital in Wheeling having a baby."

"Hello," answered Judy.

"Yo," said Thurston. He had just played the fifteenth hole. "What's up?"

"Cathy's water broke, and Jon took her to the hospital. I'm on my way to Wheeling now," said Judy as she fastened her seat belt.

"Okay, I'll drive straight to the hospital from here. I'll stop and get a sandwich on the way. I'll see you there."

When Thurston got to the hospital, Cathy had already delivered. It was August 1, and he was looking at a seven-pound, thirteen-ounce baby boy, who was the most pleasant and satisfying sight he had ever seen. Thurston had never had a son himself. He hugged Cathy and Jon and congratulated them on creating such a big, strong, handsome baby boy. Thurston gleamed with admiration as he reached to pick up his newborn grandson.

"He will call me grandfather," Thurston proudly said with an assured smile.

"Don't worry, Dad," said Cathy. "We're going to have Riley Giuseppe put on the birth certificate, not Zeppy Riley. I know you were really concerned about that."

"Thank God," said Thurston. "I had to live my whole life with my name, Thurston, which I hated. Oh, Jon, don't forget we're playing in that United Way golf scramble at Williams Country Club on the fifteenth of August. Sparky Simcox and Floyd Braun make up our foursome. I also talked to Judy's cousin, Joe Caironich, and he's sure he has you a job lined up at Parker Industries in Ashtabula, Ohio. We can check on that in the next couple of weeks."

"Wow, I hope so," said Jon. "I'm not crazy about working the night shift at the Hampton for the rest of my life. I already turned in my notice, and Cathy and I are temporarily moving in with my mom and Joe in Weirton."

Joe Van Lorne, Jon's father, graduated from the School of Law at Harvard University in Cambridge, Massachusetts, and worked with his business partner Ed Lagula. Their office was located in downtown Weirton; Joe and Kate lived in Crambell Addition on Weirton Heights with their son Joey and their grandson Joseph. Their two-story stately house was immaculate as it stood along a row of picture perfect estate homes. Joe was very meticulous about his lawn. Every blade of grass stood like a soldier at attention.

Joe's father, Joseph, was French Canadian and lived in Montréal, Canada. His mom had passed away a year ago.

Jon and Catherine moved in with the Van Lorne's for a few weeks, but Catherine and Rie Guy spent most of their time with Judy at the Beltow's. Jon was renting a motel room in Ashtabula, Ohio, while trying out his new job at Parker Industries. Jon had a previous injury in an auto accident that injured his arm. His work required assembly of parts, which was not impossible but was difficult, because of the different positioning of his arms. The constant repetition brought on a lot of pain. The doctor prescribed a potent pain medicine for some relief, and Jon continued to work with no pain. Jon and Catherine always loved the Lake Erie area and were searching for an apartment for the three of them. They moved into an apartment complex in Ashtabula, which had two upstairs bedrooms with a handrail with wide openings. They installed a mesh netting to keep Rie Guy from falling through. All was finally safe and satisfied Judy, who was terrified.

Jon joined a softball team, which he would eventually manage, and he and Thurston found a couple of golf courses that were a little challenging but enjoyable to play.

Catherine was pleased because they were close to Geneva-on-the-Lake, Ohio, where her family vacationed every year. Thurston would rent a small cottage on the lake close to the beach. He would renew the rental every year in advance. Catherine and her sisters would reminisce about the times going to Allen's Store, Eddie's

Grille, Mary's Italian Restaurant, the amusement park, and every day fun in the sun. Those were memories that can never be taken away. She was hoping that they could create many more memories living in the area.

CHAPTER 14

Catherine and Judith schemed together a belated wedding reception, and a first birthday party for Riley. What a perfect plan. On August 1, 1999, it all took place at the Beltow's new home. Jon had invited friends from work and softball, along with more the two hundred other guests. Rie Guy was totally the center of attention because never was there such an attractive child. Rie Guy loaded up with an outlandish amount of gifts, and so did Mom and Dad. Thurston had drunk too many beers and lemon drops with tequila that he ended up on the living room couch. He was passed out with a beer and an uneaten sandwich on his chest. Jon informed Thurston that he got smart with the police at 2:00 am and told them, "The party's over when it's over."

Well, the party was over in about fifteen more minutes. Judy and Cathy thanked everyone for coming and for the gifts. The money gifts, along with some money that Jon and Cathy had saved in a year and a half, enabled them to put a down payment on a house in Ashtabula, Ohio. Cathy was elated. The "Ashtabula Cottage" was a beautiful two-bedroom home facing Lake Erie in a most spectacular fashion. It had two large windows in the living room that enveloped the view. The bathroom was small, but Jon and Thurston increased the size and installed a whirlpool bathtub. Rie Guy was two years old and was already spitting out computer jargon and singing almost complete songs. Judy and Thurston were amazed at his abilities.

"There is something very special about this boy, and I am on the verge of knowing," said Thurston, lighting up a cigarette and blowing a smoke ring.

"Who do you think you are, the wizard? You know two things: nothing and completely nothing," said Judy.

"I'm new, but I'm not brand new. I wasn't born yesterday, you know."

"Could have fooled me," said Judy.

"Different strokes for different folks, get it, I say tomato…"

"You say tomato…I say shut up!" replied Judy, smiling at him.

"Fuge" was the closest Rie Guy got to calling Thurston grandfather. Judy was called Mimi because she and Riley looked so much alike. Austin Powers, who became Rie Guy's favorite actor, who created Dr. Evil (me and Minnie Me): Mimi. Rie Guy began patting Fuge on the head lightly.

"Grrrrrr," growled Fuge. "You're bugging me Rie Guy, you better give it a rest. You better put a lid on it. You're jumping on my last nerve, that's it." Thurston grabbed Rie Guy and repeatedly kissed him on the back of the neck and said, "You had enough?" If Rie guy said no, he got more kisses.

Rie Guy was so happy with the new home. It had a shared private beach where Cathy and Rie Guy spent all their time. Rie Guy lived in a pair of shorts the entire summer, and he would stay a golden copper brown. Cathy taught him everything about the lake, about the rocks, about all the vegetation, about the trees (a real tree hugger), and about Geneva-on-the-Lake and the surrounding area. They would take walks everywhere.

Thurston and Judy took Rie Guy on many adventure trips to Geauga Lake, Sea World, and a few amusement parks in the Lake Erie area. Rie Guy thought that they, Mimi and Fuge, owned a whole chain of Holiday Inns. Rie Guy loved the Holiday Inns, the swimming pools, the Jacuzzis, and the vending machines. He had his way at the Holiday Inn.

In the summer of the year 2000, Mimi and Fuge stayed with Rie Guy at the "Ashtabula Cottage." Jon and Catherine had gone away for the day. Rie Guy was in love. A girl from over a couple of streets rode her bicycle and stopped to see Rie Guy every day. She was two years older and blond.

Rie Guy had a soft spot in his heart for blonds. Her name was Marylyn. He adored her and couldn't keep his eyes off her.

"I cooked something," said Mimi. "Marylyn, can you come and eat with Rie Guy?"

She said thanks but she was going back home and got on her bicycle. Rie Guy did not want her to leave and was in a panic. Marylyn pedaled down the street and Rie Guy ran after her with no shirt and no shoes, screaming, "I love you! I love you! I love you!" hobbling because the alley was gravel.

"Come back here," yelled Thurston, waving for him to come back.

Rie Guy returned with his head down and crushed. The love of his life had left. He had a very heavy heart. He came in the house with the most contorted and anguished face.

"What's wrong, Rie Guy?" Mimi asked, being a caring grandmother.

"You make me so sad." He cried, making the ugliest face possible.

"Marylyn's coming back after she eats."

Rie Guy sat up with a big smile and said, "She loves me!"

CHAPTER 15

Jon, Thurston, Sparky, and Dennis Crane were getting ready for a day of golf at Pleasant Valley Country Club. Thurston had helped pay off the twenty-thousand-dollar–fine that was put on Jon by the president of the United States. Jon still didn't seem happy about how things were going with the government, and Thurston could sense it. Jon was a little despondent.

"What's eating you, Jon?" asked Thurston.

Sparky was singing a Frank Sinatra song about regrets and how he did all that. "Do you remember when we did all that, Jon?" asked Sparky. "I don't regret doing any of it."

"You're right, Sparky," said Jon. "We did all that, at the power plant, for nothing. The United States is getting worse. It's all about the new president and their precious oil."

"Why do you say that?" asked Thurston.

"This is the way I see it. Our presence in the Middle East is very disturbing to those countries. We have occupied space in Saudi Arabia since Operation Desert

Thurston and Sparky, mysteriously, happened to like the same singing legends that spanned over many, many years, Frank Sinatra and Bob Dylan.

Thurston and Sparky both loved karaoke, and the Pleasant Valley Country Club had a disc jockey, Dick Clarick, every other Thursday night. Dick Clarick didn't have any hard rock music with karaoke, but he did have the oldies, that Thurston and Sparky loved. They would take their turn and sing their hearts out, forever singing Sinatra and Dylan songs. Thurston got through the songs, but Sparky Simcox was great. He would sound exactly like the artist. One time in Ashtabula, Jon, Sparky, and Thurston went to a bar that was advertising karaoke. Sparky had knocked everyone's socks off when he sang "New York, New York" by Frank Sinatra. Sparky went into the restroom and stood at the urinal next to a drunkin' fool, who was repeating the New York song very badly. The drunk looked at Sparky and said, "You don't like my singing?"

Sparky could see out of the corner of his eye that Jon was at the mirror, combing his black, wavy, European hair. Jon noticed that this drunkin' slob was now pissing on Sparky's shoe.

"That's a sign of a good shoe," Sparky said calmly. "You piss on it, and my sock doesn't get wet!" At that same moment, Sparky gave him a punch, right on his lips.

"Asshole," yelled Jon, grabbing him by his scruffy hair from behind and dragged him to an empty toilet stall, pushed him in, and they put the boots to him. They kicked his arms and legs until he pleaded for them to stop. They left the restroom quickly, grabbed Thurston, beer and all, and got the hell out of there. They knew they were due for an ass-kicking as soon as someone went in the restroom. Needless to say, they never went back to that karaoke bar.

CHAPTER 16

"I've got to give Pinka a call, she's close to having her baby," complained Cathy as she picked up her phone and gave it to Judy and continued to the sink with coffee cups and saucers. "Can you hit her number? I haven't been keeping up very well. Isn't she due in May?"

"Uh-huh…Pinka?" asked Judy as she smiled and winked at Cathy. "Your long-lost sister wants to talk to you. She hasn't called you in, what, at least two months. Does she even know that you're eight months pregnant?"

"Give me that phone, Mom," Cathy exclaimed. "How are you doing, Pinka? I'll bet you look like a beach ball. Aren't you due in May?"

"Yeah," said Pinka. "Thanks for the sympathy."

Pinka finally finished her degree in psychology at West Virginia University and got hired at Ruby Hospital as a psychologist. Mike was now a partial owner of a construction company (Huge Structural and Home Improvement) in Morgantown, which was solely owned by an ambitious entrepreneur, Howard Huge. Howard and Mike would give estimates and take on projects. They did anything from installing structural steel buildings to designer improvements to private residential homes.

Cathy and Pinka continued talking while Judy took Rie Guy into the living room where Jon and Thurston were drinking beer and watching the Pittsburgh Steelers playing football.

Thurston was trying to light a cigarette with his new lighter and was having difficulty. Judy took it off of him and said, "You have to hold this part down, after you strike the flint. Its child and idiot proof."

"What's you talkin' bout, idiot proof? How you know so much about it, fool?" asked Thurston with his lips puckered.

"If the shoe fits, wear it," snickered Judy, patting him on the back. "I light birthday candles, and I have a lighter just like that in my kitchen, dummy."

"I want to watch Austin Powers," pouted Rie Guy as he grabbed his Austin Powers VCR tape from a huge selection of tapes.

"No way," replied Thurston. "How does he do that? I wouldn't be able to find that tape. Two and a half years old, and he's a genius. There is something real special about that boy. I'm dead serious. Anyhow, no way, you have to wait until the game is over." He grabbed some potato chips and took a big swallow of beer.

"Forget it, big guy," demanded Jon. "The Steelers are down by three points in the fourth quarter against their number one rival, Oakland. Don't bother us!"

"Thank you for the help, if we need anything else, we'll just ask, okay!" replied Judy, picking up Rie Guy and going back into the kitchen. Rie Guy was sticking his tongue out at them.

"So the sonogram shows a boy," stated Cathy as she pointed to the bathroom, signaling her mom to put Riley on the potty chair. He was having a rough time with that. "I remember having Riley, Pinka. Jon did not want a soldier. Now he's elated. Dad is crazy about Rie Guy. That's what they call him, Rie Guy. It's good to have a firstborn son, you know, for that manly ego. Yeaah,"

"Tell me!" said Pinka, taking a deep breath. "Mike is overexcited." She paused a second because Mike was coming in the door. "Hi, Mike, I didn't cook anything, so stick something in the microwave, all right," she said, pointing toward the kitchen. "Cathy, I'm back. You'll have to forgive me, but I have to lie down for a while, this baby is getting heavy."

"Bye, I don't know if Jon and I will be around when what's-his-name is born. Mom and Dad will be there. You can count on them."

"It's Samuel Earl, smarty, bye."

The Pittsburgh Steelers made a field goal in overtime to beat Oakland. Thank God.

"Rie Guy," yelled Jon. "You can put your Austin Powers tape in now. The games over, Pittsburgh won."

Thurston had to go to the bathroom for what seemed like the tenth time. Everyone knows how that is when you're drinking beer. He said to Jon, "These pants are like a cheap hotel."

"Why's that, Thurston?"

"No ballroom."

They both laughed, and Jon asked, "You think maybe that beer belly has anything to do with that?"

"Hey, Judy keeps shrinking my pants," trying to get his fingers between his stomach and his waste band of his jogging outfit, not being very successful.

"Go ahead, Mom, Jon will help Riley with the VCR. I have to call Vicky and tell her about Pinka's baby being a boy, and the baby's name."

"Vicky, long time no talk. What's happening? Look at you. You're in the city with a million apartments, townhouses, and multimillion dollar homes, in Woodbridge, Virginia." She was thinking how lucky her youngest sister was to be making huge money and having a million outlets for clothing and everything you could possibly need.

"You're missing two things, Cathy, the rent is high, and the living isn't cheap, if you have any idea what I'm saying. I don't know how long I can stay here with the cost of living being so high. I miss mom and dad. I haven't had much luck with men. I'm doing e-mail with a couple of toads, but not many frogs that would turn into a prince. Get it. I've tried so hard to get into the Pittsburgh, Pennsylvania, school system. My dream has always been to live in Robinson Township at Chestnut Ridge Apartments. By the way, I bought me a little puppy, his name is Winston. He's a genuine miniature Yorkshire terrier with papers. I know who his mom and dad are. He's so cute. How's my Riley Giuseppe?"

"He's good, getting smarter. You won't believe this little guy. Dad is infatuated with him. He was walking at eight months, messes with the computer. I mean he says web addresses, yellowtruck.com, that kind of crap. He watches entire movies, and sings entire songs. What do you think about that?" bragged Cathy, taking a minute to catch her breath.

"Sounds like me when I was young," replied Vicky, also bragging.

"Anyhow, the reason I called was to tell you that Pinka's having a boy, and his name is going to be Samuel Earl."

"Great! Grandma Beltow will like that, because Earl is her brother's name," remarked Vicky, yawning a little.

"Am I keeping you awake, I'm not that boring," laughed Cathy, sneezing at the same time.

"God bless you, no, I've had a few late nights, you know, thinking about what to do, the school year is almost over."

"Just leave, stay with Mom and Dad until you find something in Pittsburgh. Don't drive yourself nuts thinking about it."

"You're probably right. I'll have to think about it, I have to get out of my lease. Not to worry, I'll do it, bye."

"Bye," finished Cathy as she went to check on Rie Guy.

Rie Guy was in a terminal stair watching Austin Powers. He would not look away from the screen. He had watched that particular Austin Powers video at least two hundred times from beginning to end. Judy and Thurston had never seen such concentration; you could not get his attention. His eyes were glued to the screen; he knew this Austin Powers adventure by heart.

"No doubt in my mind. That Rie Guy is a God-sent mastermind!" bragged Thurston.

CHAPTER 17

Thurston was back on the computer, looking up information about Catherine of Aragon, who was born into a family of kings and queens on December 16, 1485, in Alcala de Hernares, Spain. She was the daughter of Queen Isabella of Castile and mighty King Ferdinard of Aragon in Spain and was destined to become a queen herself. She was betrothed at four years old to the future king of England. She fulfilled this destiny but became victim of Henry VIII inability to produce a male heir to the throne. Henry was obsessed with producing a male heir to continue the Tudor dynasty. Queen Catherine bore six children; only one survived. That was Princess Mary, who later became Queen Mary I of England. Unable to produce a male heir, she was removed from her throne after twenty-four years, and the marriage was annulled, although she certainly left her mark in history. Thurston stated that King Henry VIII sure had his way with the women. After the annulment, he married five more times. He beheaded two of his wives for being unfaithful, but his third wife, Queen Jane Seymour, produced his "Prince of Wales." (Queen Jane Seymour died a few days after giving birth, widely believed to be following birth complications.)

"I can't find what I'm looking for about Queen Catherine's death. It's like I'm trying to empty an Olympic-size swimming pool with a teaspoon. I'm pulling on a string, and there's no end."

"Would you give it a rest," exclaimed Judy. "What is so important about what you're searching for anyhow? All this England stuff is getting totally boring," as she made a motion as if she was yawning.

"I'm telling you, there was something in what that Queen Catherine wrote. I've got to find it," as he kept doing searches to find that letter.

"You are nuttier then a fruitcake. Would you just put a lid on it!" said Judy as she stretched out on the couch to watch some television. Thurston had a way of constantly bugging Judy, flapping his lips all the time.

"Yeah, yeah," said Thurston, thumbing his nose at her.

"Don't forget that we're going to the Pittsburgh Speedway tonight to watch KJ," as she gave him a "you forgot" look.

"You must think I was born yesterday. I was just checking to see if you remembered." replied Thurston, actually not remembering that they had planned on going to the races, since it was Saturday.

Judith's brother, "K," and his wife, Elizabeth, lived in Ohio, and had three children, KJ, Tara, and Emily. The Mueller's had gotten into car racing because they had sent their son, KJ, to Universal NASCAR Tech, in North Carolina, for the Automotive Technology Training

Program, where he would become an in-demand auto technician. The core program trained him to troubleshoot, service, and repair domestic automobiles. North Carolina was very heavy with auto racing known as (NASCAR) the National Association of Stock Car Auto Racing, which is a family-owned and operated business venture that sanctions and governs multiple auto racing sports events. *NASCAR* is second only to the National Football League amongst professional sports franchises in terms of television ratings in the United States. KJ quickly became a genius with motors and transmissions. He became infatuated with car racing. He was quickly hired by a Ford dealership in Washington, Pennsylvania. Shortly afterward, he purchased an E-modified race car; 4m was KJ's number. He began racing at the Greater Pittsburgh Speedway and became "Rookie of the Year" in his first year of racing. His father, "K," and his brother-in-law, Rick, was his pit crew. It was an expensive hobby without sponsors. He received petty money's from his aunts and uncles, which he appreciated, but tires were one hundred dollars apiece, engine, ten thousand. He needed big cash from big companies. It was very competitive, and you had to be in the winning circle contentiously. KJ raced every Saturday, unless it rained. He had support from his own immediate family, a few friends, and Judith and Thurston.

"Look at that, It's spectacular at night," Thurston would say as he thought; many people have never seen or heard anything like that; the sound of the motors was deafening. He would see 4m flashing by—most fantastic thing Thurston had ever seen.

"Oh my God, I found it," yelled Thurston. "I found the letter."

CHAPTER 18

Jon and Judge Clydesdale III were engaged in a telephone conversation, and Judge was filling Jon in on what had been happening with him and Hoy Lee Chong Grant. Hoy Lee Chong was now working as an engineer at Cleveland's NASA Glenn Research Center and Dayton's air force research lab.

"I'm not into all that technical research and development, you know me. So through a few friends that I met, which includes Jude Yamin, the past president's friend who got me here in the first place, hooked me up with a job. I'm doing great. I am now a bartender, making huge money in tips. Do you believe that?"

"What kind of place are we talking? Is it downtown Chicago?" asked Jon, wondering how Judge pulled this one off. He could fall in crap and come out smelling like a rose.

"It's called Rock Bottom. It's a casual beer drinking bar that sits above State Street and Grand Avenue. A little tacky yet refined. It has a tiki hut décor with house brew or specialty cocktails. Great food to keep your belly satisfied. I'm loving it."

"It didn't take you birds long to get on top," remarked Jon. "I miss all the fun and excitement that went on at Rocky's and at the nuclear power plant in Stockton, Pennsylvania."

"Yeah, I'm still paying on the twenty-thousand-dollar-fine that the past president put on me. Wait, Jon, I'm getting Hoy Lee Chong on a three-way conversation."

"All right, I'll wait."

"Jon, are you there, Chong's on the line," said Judge after hooking up the three ways.

"Hoy Lee Chong, I see you got yourself a big Job in Cleveland, or is it Dayton?" Jon said, smiling.

"Oh, have velly fine job," answered Chong. "Just kidding, Sparky always got upset when I talked broken Chinese. I actually work at both places. I have to travel between Cleveland and Dayton. Our Dayton Research Lab will be helping test an alternative fuel as part of a future, multimillion dollar Green Planet Infusion Mission. If the fuel performs as hoped, it could pave the way for cheaper, cleaner satellites and spacecraft. The demonstration mission aims to fly a small unmanned spacecraft with modified thrusters powered by an experimental alternative fuel. Isn't that interesting?"

"That's as clear as mud, and totally boring. You've become a for-real freaking nerd since we split. What happened to your freaking backbone? We should take that freaking Green Planet Mission spacecraft hostage so we can talk to the governor of Ohio and the new president," responded Jon, laughing out load.

"I don't think we would be so lucky a second time, they would put us away, forever," yelled Judge as he interrupted that conversation.

"We were lucky to get out of that mess we created at the nuclear power plant, Judge. We risked everything trying to prove a point. The sad part is the United States is becoming more of a target. This new president will definitely get us into war by keeping our troops in Saudi Arabia because of that stinking oil. All he is doing is pissing Osama Bin Laden off," said Jon, thinking that the United States of America better get some respect before they get attacked again.

"You will never change, Jon. You were born to be wild. Okay, nice talking to you, but I have to go back to work. Bye," replied Hoy Lee Chong as he hung up the receiver.

"By the way, Judge, Zeppy Riley is growing up to be quite a character," replied Jon, finishing the conversation.

"That boy is going to be famous someday," replied Judge. "Jon, I hope we can hook up some day and have a couple of beers. I can tell you more about my new job."

"Spare me, I'm so freaking jealous. Bye."

"Bye," said Judge, breaking the connection.

Jon was so happy for his friends, who were part of the original Rocky's Alley Ratts. He, in some mysterious way, felt proud of what they had accomplished.

CHAPTER 19

On the morning of September 11, 2001, terrorists from the Islamist militant group Al-Qaeda hijacked four commercial planes and attempted to fly them into several United States targets. The attacks were a series of coordinated suicide attacks upon New York City and Washington, DC. The hijackers intentionally flew two of those planes, American Airlines Flight 11 and United Airlines Flight 175 into the north and south towers of the World Trade Center complex in New York City; both towers collapsed within two hours. The hijackers also intentionally crashed American Airlines Flight 77 into the Pentagon in Arlington, Virginia, and intended to crash a fourth hijacked plane, United Airlines Flight 93, into the United States Capitol Building in Washington, DC; however, the plane crashed into a field near Shanksville, Pennsylvania, after its passengers attempted to take control of the plane from the hijackers.

Thurston was walking up the steps of their split-level home in Weirton when he heard on the television that a small piper cub plane had hit one of the towers of the

World Trade Center. Not paying much attention to what was happening on TV, he continued up the second flight of steps to his bedroom. They started having a special news report about it being a larger plane that crashed into Tower One of the World Trade Center at 8:46 am. It got Thurston's attention. He began watching as a second plane crashed into Tower Two at 9:04 am.

"Unbelievable, you got to be shitting me, we are under attack," thought Thurston as he grabbed his cell phone and punched in Judy's number. She had just gone to the store.

"Hello," answered Judy at that moment entering the store.

"Where are you? I'm thinking that we're under attack, by terrorists," exclaimed Thurston. "Airplanes are crashing into the World Trade Center in New York."

"Whoa, whoa, slow down. What's happening?"

"I don't know what's happening. It's on television right now, a special report. You aren't going to believe this. Another plane just crashed into the Pentagon. Hey, get back here as soon as you can until we find out what's happening."

"On my way," said Judy as she was hurrying through the parking lot get back to her car. Thurston was punching in Jon's cell number. Jon was at work, but Thurston was sure that he would be watching this develop on TV.

"Hello, Thurston. Yeah, you know I'm watching. Didn't I tell you this was going to happen? They've been using our airlines. They are hijacking our planes."

"You think. Like committing suicide, crashing those planes on suicide missions."

"That's the way I'm seeing it. I wonder how many more they have hijacked? We'll soon find out, I guess," Jon said casually.

"Look, 10:05 am. Another plane just went down. They said somewhere in Pennsylvania."

"I'm wondering where our president is right now, Thurston. He sure as hell needs to be alerted."

"Probably getting his toe nails manicured or playing golf."

"Something important like that," replied Jon as he was switching though the channels on the television to see if he could pick up anything different. "I'm really curious about what this country is going to do. These people are such wimps that are running this country. Look, Thurston, the plane that went down in Pennsylvania. After the passengers revolted, the hijackers crashed the plane into the ground near Shanksville, Pennsylvania. They're saying it was targeted for either the Capitol building in Washington, or the White House."

"All right, Jon, I'll check with you later. Judy's coming. I called her and told her to get her ass home. Later." Thurston hung up.

"Why is someone doing this? They are killing thousands of people. I'm scared, Thurston," asked Judy as she was putting purse down and hugging Thurston. "Are we safe?"

"I believe it's over for now, nothing else has happened. Then his smile hardened, his expression intensified, anger was churning in his stomach, as he thought, "Osama bin Laden…Dead!"

Suspicion quickly fell on the Al-Qaeda, naturally, knowing that Osama bin Laden would deny any involvement. The president immediately called for all civilized nations to band together and fight terrorism. The military of the United States mobilized for war in the operation code named Enduring Freedom. The government declared Osama bin Laden to be the main suspect and sent the military to fight him and his terrorist organization called Al-Qaeda in Afghanistan. The military had been able to capture numerous leaders within the terrorist organization but had not been able to capture bin Laden himself.

CHAPTER 20

Thurston finally got to continue looking at the letter that was left by the once queen of England because of her marriage to Henry VIII. Catherine of Aragon was very much the ideal queen. She was supportive of her husband, and like him, she enjoyed music and dance. Not being able to produce a male heir, the archbishop of Canterbury declared the twenty-four–year marriage of Henry VIII and Catherine null and void on March 30, 1534. Catherine was given a new title of "Dowager Princess of Wales" although some still addressed her as queen. She was sent away to live out her days in remote Kimbolton Castle, and this was only further exasperated by the fact that she was forbidden to see her daughter, Mary. She wrote many letters. Sensing that her end was near, Catherine wrote to Henry one more time.

"Listen to this, Judy," sputtered Thurston, trying to make some sense out of the letter. "It's written in Old English or something. She says in the hour of her death that she still has tender love and commends herself to Henry to safeguard his soul. She says that his preference, before worldly matters, and the pampering of his body was to cast her into many calamities and himself into many troubles. She says for her part, she pardons him everything. Get it. She was completely forgiving him, and furthermore, praying that God will pardon him also. She says she bore him six children, and only one survived. Princess Mary. She later says, 'I commend unto you our daughter Mary, beseeching thou to be a good father, as she had desired.' Catherine wishes her servants to get the wages due them and year more. The part that is more riddling and puzzling. She says in the following centuries to come a firstborn son will be born to Catherine of Cheshire, a firstborn daughter, of a firstborn son, of a firstborn daughter, of a firstborn son. He would be thou Prince, thou King, Lord Henry, in a future time, and he shall share the powers of royalty and acquire mind strengths beyond those of all worldly beings, a savior of mankind. Sir Zep"

Judy was completely stunned with Thurston continually digging into all that English garbage. It seemed so trivial. She could see him weighing and balancing, looking for some mysterious answer. She believed there was a figure in a red suit, presumably the devil, directing him. He was driving her crazy. She decided to put an end to the subject permanently.

"Will you stop making all of that crap up," said Judy, protesting. "You are spooking me. No one really cares what the hell Catherine said or did in the past. You got to get back into the real world and stop humiliating yourself. Enough is enough, you adorable hunk. Start paying more attention to your beautiful wife."

"I will, I will," shrieked Thurston. The wheels were turning in Thurston's head. He left what he was doing and went over to Judy to give her a kiss. As he bent over, she accidently sneezed in Thurston's face. He said "God bless you" as he blinked his eyes and wiped his hand across his face. "Do you serve towels with your showers?" growled Thurston. He was laughing as he got her a tissue from the end table.

"I'm sorry, Thurston," said Judy, giving him a kiss. "I guess I should let you do what you want to do. Are you hungry?"

"Not right now, maybe a little later," said Thurston, hurrying back to what he was doing and wanting to find out about Catherine of Cheshire. He remembered tracing his mom's ancestry to a John Blackshaw, of Chester, Cheshire, England. He began putting it together that Cathy's ancestors were originally from Cheshire County. Cathy's first name is Catherine, thus Catherine of Cheshire. Rie Guy is her firstborn son; it all fits. It continues to say that Catherine was the firstborn daughter of a firstborn son of a firstborn daughter of a firstborn son. *My God, I can't believe it. It's coming all together. Catherine Michelle is my firstborn daughter. I am the firstborn son of my mom, Oscea Madrid Blackshaw. She is the firstborn of my grandfather, O. W. Blackshaw, who is the firstborn of my great-grandfather, T. O. Blackshaw.*

Oscea, Thurston's mom, was married to Thurston J. Beltow II, who had worked as a truck driver in Weirton Steel Corporation. He was also a builder, along with his brother, Gopher Beltow, who worked for a huge contractor, Donald Trompit. Donald was a developer who took on contracts to build residential homes in Weirton, West Virginia. Thurston II and Gopher worked there on their off hours from Weirton Steel Corporation. O. W. Blackshaw, Oscea's father, was an ambitious entrepreneur who had many different businesses in Gilmer County, West Virginia. He owned and operated a grocery store, which was also the post office. He owned Blackshaw's Esso Service Station on the corner of US Route 33 and Route 119, in which his son, Golden, managed and operated. He also owned a large building in which he turned into a prosperous roller skating rink. His son also managed the roller rink.

Thomas Oscar Blackshaw, O. W's father, was a carpenter by trade. He made his living doing makeshift jobs for anyone who needed something built out of wood, including additions to homes, such as porches or extra space rooms.

Thurston couldn't believe what he was deciphering. He was showing and explaining it to Judy, who was starting to sense that maybe Thurston had dug up something about Rie Guy, whether it made any good sense or not.

"This fantastic story has a huge resemblance to our bloody family," Thurston blurted out stupidly with a perfect English accent.

"I wonder what all that means about sharing the powers of royalty and the mind strength, and most of all, the savior of mankind. We have to keep this all silent from Jon and Cathy until we see what occurs as Rie Guy grows up. Are you with me, Thurston?"

"Well, I've had suspicions about Rie Guy being something out of the ordinary. No doubt that he is much smarter then the average person just by his actions. We'll watch how he grows, and if he is here on earth for a special purpose or to change any course of history, we'll just have to wait and watch," replied Thurston, thinking how incredible it really was that his grandson would be gifted with so many powers.

"Right," agreed Judy, wide-eyed, and smiling at Thurston. "We just wait and watch."

CHAPTER 21

Riley Giuseppe (Zeppy Riley) Van Lorne was a walking miracle. He had begun his school years in the Ashtabula School District. It was the year 2004 in the fall, and school was so exciting to Rie Guy. Cathy always knew that Rie Guy was gifted, but never realized to what degree. By the time he was two-and-a-half, he was reciting the alphabet backward and forward and calculating mathematical equations in his head. He had reached the milestones of walking and talking at eight months. He could speak full sentences and read by the time he was three. He always had a strong desire to explore, investigate, and master the environment with the help of his mother. He could distinguish between reality and fantasies, such as questions about Santa Clause and the Tooth Fairy. Her worry was that he would be completely bored with the normal movement of the educational system. His teacher was amazed that he talked and carried himself like a grown adult. He could actually carry on a conversation, a genius.

He liked the idea of going on the school bus with the other kids until some of the older boys started bullying. Life became a little trying. Cathy approached the bus driver and asked what he could do. He said that the most he could do is confront the bullies and tell them to leave Rie Guy alone, but he said that sometimes it makes things worse. Cathy found out the names of the bullies and turned them in to the principal. Nothing changed, and Rie Guy was starting to not like school. She was appalled and decided to change things. To give Rie Guy the opportunity to be all that he could be, Cathy had decided that it is time that she makes good use of her education. She applied and drove to Florida to interview for the government jobs that were advertised and was accepted as a regional biologist with the Florida Conservation Commission in the Invasive Plant Management Section. Jon was having a lot of trouble performing his job because of his arm and was all right with moving to Florida. He would find employment there that wasn't so painful. Cathy had talked it over with her two sisters, and they agreed that she should accept the job. Pinka's son, Samuel, was four years old now and had gained a little sister, Anna, who was as cute as a button. Victoria left her job in Woodbridge, Virginia, and had been working as a reading specialist for Hancock County Schools in West Virginia and was staying with Judy and Thurston, "Mimi and Fuge," for a couple of years until she could find a teaching job in Pittsburgh. She also had a part-time job at a restaurant in Robinson Township where she was planning on getting an apartment. Cathy accepted the Florida job and was to report to work the day after Christmas.

Christmas was always a special time at MiMi's house; Rie Guy would call it Christmas in the kitchen. All the families would gather on Christmas day in Mimi and Fuge's kitchen, which had a huge extension sunroom surrounded with windows and doors. Dennis Crane had built this beautiful scenic room, which extended onto a double-tier deck after the Beltow's had purchased their home in Weirton. Santa Clause came because the sleigh bells could be heard from the inside of the Beltow's home on Christmas Eve. All the kids would run and hide and want to get in their beds and cover up their heads. There wasn't another sound.

Christmas morning always appeared to be close to a Norman Rockwell picture: presents were carefully arranged under the Christmas tree in perfect order, snow was flurrying as snowflakes danced beautifully and uniquely on the outside of the windows. It was quiet and sullen for that moment. Anna had fallen asleep on a little couch next to the small table that held Santa's milk and cookies. Thurston was staring at the overstuffed stockings that were hanging, and how they brought a fantastic glow of happiness. Someone had written: There is nothing sadder in the world than to awaken Christmas morning and not be a child. It all abruptly ended as Anna woke up and was squealing and yelling for everyone to get up. Aunt Cathy was on her way to Florida, so Aunt Pinka was assigned to pass out the presents. Thurston turned on the Television and *A Christmas Story* was on as they opened their gifts, Scut Farcus was terrorizing Ralphie, and Randy was flat on his back, saying, "I can't get up." Rie Guy and Samuel loved that story and said every line before they said it on TV. Judy's father had once bought her a manger scene that lit up, and Thurston would every year put it on a separate table. Any time the kids would pass it, Thurston would make them say, "Happy birthday, Jesus."

Judy's father, Harold, was always there for Christmas. His grandchildren always knew him and his wife, Anna Marie, as "Nanny and Pap." Anna passed away in January of 1998 and never got to see any of her great-grandchildren. Harold retired from Weirton Steel Corporation as an overhead crane operator. The grandkids all adored Nanny and Pap, and they vacationed with them every year at Geneva-on-the-Lake, Ohio.

Rie Guy loved that everyone would come, Judy's two brothers, Uncle "K" and Elizabeth, KJ, Terra and David, Emily and Rick, and sometimes Uncle Harold. Thurston's two brothers, Uncle Levi and Elaine, and Uncle Lawrence and Mary. Of course, Jon, Uncle Mike, and Aunt "Enie," which the kids all called Victoria, and Winston, the miniature Yorkshire terrier who now lived at Mimi and Fuge's house. Grandma and Grandpa Beltow were also there.

Cathy arrived in Florida on the day after Christmas. She was staying at the Holiday Inn and had started her job. The plan was that Jon and Rie guy would come down a little later. Thurston and Judy had packed up Thurston's truck with everything from the "Ashtabula Cottage" and were also planning a trip to Florida. Jon and Cathy had a realtor working on renting the cottage while they were living in Florida. Cathy quickly rented a house in Florida and had a mattress and box spring delivered with some of the money from Jon's 401(k) that they had cashed. By the end of January 2005, they were completely settled in, and Jon had landed a job in Winter Haven as an assistant pro at Lake Regions Golf and Yacht Club in Winter Haven, Florida. That pleased Thurston because they would have a place to golf when he and Judy would visit. They had also found a renter for the "Ashtabula Cottage."

CHAPTER 22

In November of 2005, Jon and Thurston were playing their first round of golf at the Lake Region Golf Club in Winter Haven, Florida. Thurston knew that Jon was a little undecided about what the president of the United States was doing in the Middle East.

"Do you remember the huge controversy that arose when the president sent troops into Iraq in 2003 claiming that the country led by Saddam Hussein was developing weapons of mass destruction and aiding Al-Qaeda operatives? Time passed, and there was no evidence of those weapons found in Iraq and no tie to the Al-Qaeda forces. People argued, and I agreed that the Iraq War drew attention away from the war in Afghanistan."

In October, 2001, American troops were on the offensive in Afghanistan. The goal of Operation Enduring Freedom, as the mission was dubbed, was to stamp out Afghanistan's Islamic fundamentalist Taliban regime, which was aiding and abetting Al-Qaeda and its leader, Osama bin Laden, a Saudi national who lived in the Afghan hills and urged his followers to kill Americans.

The president informed the American public that 'carefully targeted action' was being carried out to crush the military capability of Al-Qaeda and the Taliban, with help from British, Canadian, Australian, German, and French troops. An additional forty nations around the world provided intelligence as well as bases from which the operations were conducted. He vowed to continue to take what he called the war on terror to any country that sponsored, harbored, or trained terrorists.

"What upsets me is that they can't get their hands on that piece of shit, Osama bin Laden. He has openly admitted and claimed responsibility for the 911 attack on New York City. That man has got to be stopped," shouted Thurston as he swung his golf club and hit a beautiful drive.

"Nice hit, Thurston, the way I see it, if we keep screwing around in the Middle East, and pissing those people off, they will retaliate. I don't know what you think of Nostradamus or his predictions, but he predicted that the sky will burn at forty-five degrees and implied that it might involve some kind of horrible weapon, possibly nuclear. He referred to the great city in the new world of America near forty-five degrees latitude. Experts agree this could only be New York. Many people were thinking that he had predicted September 11, again, interpret it how you will. The sky did burn at forty-five degrees, but New York was not destroyed, nor was it a nuclear attack. If those people get nuclear arms, they will not hesitate to make New York the first target."

"Oh, yes," said Thurston in agreement about Nostradamus. "That man from the sixteenth century was quit a prophet. He predicted the rise and fall of Napoleon who was considered a butcher by his own supporters as he was exiled as emperor. He predicted the rise and fall of Adolf Hitler who was considered the greatest enemy of the human race, bloody and inhuman. He also predicted a third evil tyrant who hasn't appeared yet. Remember, the man with the blue turban who is predicted to lead his forces through Europe and start the third world war. He implied that it would involve horrible weapons, possibly nuclear. Guess what? Bullshit, Jon, I don't believe him. The Great War that has been spoken of since biblical times looks inevitable, and it appears that the countdown has started. This war that has been described as Armageddon or simply World War III is likely to be a sequence of events, a series of wars—maybe nothing. If nuclear weapons are going to be used freely, the destruction is going to be widespread and unprecedented. No part of the world is going to escape the effects and the after effects of the war. I'm quoting some of this, Jon, and you know that."

"Once there is use of nuclear weapons, it will be like giving anyone permission to use them. The UN can't stop it. US imperialism and preemptive strikes can't stop it. Only a worldwide disarmament movement can stop it," responded Jon. "Compare it to a room of people embarrassed to cough, but once one does, everyone else feels free to do so. We've both read about Nostradamus. You can't believe any of that shit. You also know that."

"I'll drink to that, Jon. I have some facts about the known nuclear nations of the world in my car. We'll look at them in the clubhouse."

Obviously becoming the foremost target of the United States…and its only dependable partner in imperial overreach, Israel…is the Middle East. Israel is especially dangerous because its leaders and supporters have made it perfectly clear for years that if they are ever devastated by any kind of war or attack, it would retaliate in indiscriminate "Samson Option" attacks against not only Muslim cities but against Europe and even Russian targets. Russia, of course, would retaliate with thousands of bombs against the United States. Any use of nuclear weapons probably would lead to rapid escalation, out-of-control spiral, to nuclear war among most of all nuclear nations "World Nuclear War."

"Look at this, Jon, the United States has 2,500 warheads on alert that can be launched immediately on any warning. We have seven thousand warheads in total at fifteen megatons [1 Mt, force of millions of tons of TNT] and a range of 8,100 miles," said Thurston, pointing at the diagram of nuclear nations. Our prime targets are Russia, China, and others. Russia is second with six thousand warheads [2,500 on alert] with the range of 6,800 miles [twenty megatons], with the US, Europe, China, and others, as prime targets. France has 464 warheads at three hundred kilotons [1 Kt, force of thousands of tons of TNT] with a range of 3,300 miles. Prime target Russia. Israel has four hundred-plus warheads with a range of five thousand miles. Prime targets Arabs/Muslim [Russia, Europe]. England has 186 warheads with the range of 7,500 miles. Prime targets Russia, China. India has 150 warheads with the range of 1,550 miles. Prime targets Pakistan, China.

Pakistan has twenty-five warheads with the range of one thousand miles. Prime targets India [Israel/US, those worms in N. Korea, unknown warheads, unknown range; prime targets, S. Korea, Japan, and United States. That is the extent of the nuclear powers of the world. I'm just showing you."

"I don't know if a worldwide disarmament is even possible," replied Jon sadly, taking a big chug of his beer. "Military disarmament is a very low priority for most nations. You and I know that the only disarmament movement that can succeed is one that will keep an arm's length from any union and to make Middle East nuclear disarmament a priority."

"Amen," shouted Thurston, adding up the scores from there very entertaining round of golf. Jon had out scored Thurston by ten strokes, naturally.

CHAPTER 23

Rie Guy had started as a midterm student at the elementary school in Bartow, Florida. He had once again loved school and was making terrific grades. Rie Guy was bigger and stronger physically, and showed the potential for performing at remarkably high levels of accomplishment when compared to the others his age. Cathy began thinking that he might need a special nurturing environment, such as a private school, to bring out all of his talents. The gifted program at the school would focus on high performance and accomplishments. It wasn't enough just to have talent. Recognizing his abilities right away, his teacher told Cathy that she had no problem keeping an eye on Riley. She told her that some gifted students are "mappers" (sequential learners), and others are leapers (spatial learners). Riley was a leaper. He was not a perfectionist or idealistic. He was a problem solver, an independent thinker, and did not mind being different from the crowd. His best traits were: he learned rapidly, he had good memorization ability, used a large vocabulary, possessed a sense of humor, and assumed responsibility. His bad traits: he was bored with underachievers and he was challenged by difficult athletic activities. He probably wouldn't play sports. Cathy decided to let him continue to participate in the regular school curriculum, because he was self-confident, and he was well-liked by his peers.

Unfortunately, the bullying started again, which upset Jon. After putting up with it for a long period of time, years, and totally disgusted, Jon said, "I'm enrolling Rie Guy in the after-school pick up program at the Olympia Tae Kwon Do Academy in Lakeland, Florida."

Tae Kwon Do is one of the most scientific Korean traditional martial arts, which teaches more than physical fighting skills. It is a discipline that shows ways of enhancing our spirit and life through training our body and mind. It became a global sport and gained an international reputation and stands among the official games of the Olympics. It is composed of three parts as shown in the English spelling, though it is one word in Korean.

Tae means "foot," "leg," or "to step on." *Kwon* means "fist" or "fight." And *Do* means the "way" or "discipline." If you put those three parts together, you can see the important concepts behind Tae Kwon Do. First, Tae Kwon Do is the right way of using "fist and feet." Second, it is a way to control or calm down fights and keep the peace. Thus Tae Kwon Do means "the right way of using all parts of the body to stop fights and help to build a better and more peaceful world." It is written.

Needless to say, with Rie Guy getting on the Tae Kwon Do pickup vehicle every day after school, the bullying stopped.

A couple of years passed, and Cathy had gotten pretty well established in her job as a biologist for the State of Florida. She had plans of purchasing a home for the three of them when the unexpected happened. She became pregnant. Whoops!

"Oh my God, Jon," cried Cathy. "I have my heart set on that house on Washingtonia Court. It's so Florida-looking, cute, and I believe the bank will loan us the full amount. I talked to my mom. She said I should hold off until the baby is born. It is the ideal Florida home that has everything I ever wanted. I hate to let it go. It's a perfect place to raise our family, and it's close to Rie Guy's school."

"Well, I think with both of us working, we should be able to take on the payment. Remember the old saying, 'Nothing ventured, nothing gained." It has a large front yard and is in an outstanding location. What is Thurston saying about all of this?"

"My dad thinks it would be a good investment because of how attractive the house is, but with me being pregnant, he thinks we should wait. I feel if the bank trusts us with the money. I'm going ahead with it."

Needless to say, they purchased the house on Washingtonia Court. Two months after the purchase of their new house, the Van Lorne's were blessed with the birth of a beautiful little daughter. October of 2007, Sahara Lola came into the world; and Cathy, Jon, and Rie Guy were elated. Cathy e-mailed a picture to Judy and Thurston. Sahara Lola was a beautiful little girl, slender and softly shaped with an adorable mild face; her skin was fair, with pink lips and twinkling eyes. Her top is strawberry blond with wild, stickum-up hair (like her mother's), which made her outstanding and the most attractive of all princesses.

Rie Guy had become interested in *Sim City*, which is an open-ended city-building computer and console video game series and the brainchild of developer Will Wright.

"Okay, Rie Guy, I guess the idea here with the city is to maintain happiness of the citizens and keeping a stable budget, right?" asked Thurston unknowingly.

"Almost, Fuge," answered Rie Guy. "It's a little more than that. First, we must define zones; each zone has limits on the kind of development that can occur there. In order to develop these zones, certain conditions must be met, such as power supply, adequate transport links, and acceptable tax levels. The residential zones provide housing, the commercial zones provide shops and offices, the industrial zones provide factories, laboratories, and farms. There are three different densities: low density for small buildings, medium density for low to mid-sized buildings, and high density for anything up to large tower blocks."

"Whoa, how do you know this, Rie guy? Who showed you how to do this?" asked Thurston, being puzzled.

"Do you remember what your favorite saying always was, Fuge, 'We learn by doing.' I learned by just doing it."

"You are amazing, what else have you learned?" asked Thurston.

"Naturally, cities must provide basic utilities, namely electricity—you know a lot about that, Fuge, being around power plants—water, and waste management. The primary source of income is taxation, which can be altered by 1 percent increments. One thing that comes out of the budget is supplying services for your citizens. These include health, education, safety, parks, and leisure. These require different buildings, where each building covers a circular range of service. Get it, Fuge?"

"I just wish I had a third of your intelligence, Rie Guy, that mind of yours is like a steel trap—unreal. What about huge malls or casinos? Those are big moneymakers for the city."

"Legalized gambling casinos, prisons, toxic waste conversion plants, and gigamalls—large shopping centers—which are big money makers, are allowed, but there could be consequences, Fuge. Business deal structures have negative effects on the city. The toxic waste dump cripples both the land value and residential desirability in the area and produces massive pollution. The prison dramatically decreases land value. The casino increases city wide crime, and the gigamall weakens demand for local commerce."

"Enough said, this is the best computer teaching tool I have ever seen, Rie Guy, but you are like a vacuum when absorbing these things. It comes so easy for you. I can't believe you have created this huge city that is very functional with no flaws."

"Did you notice the nuclear power plant that is producing all the electrical power for the city? I incorporated that because of you and my dad. Cool, huh?"

"It's cool, all right, incredible," remarked Thurston, being absolutely, unconditionally, flabbergasted by what he had just seen and heard.

CHAPTER 24

Since 2005, Thurston was working for ArcelorMittal, who had acquired Weirton Steel Corporation. In February 2004, International Steel Group entered into an asset purchase agreement with Weirton Steel Corporation. In May of 2004, International Steel Group took over the operation of Weirton Steel Corporation, becoming ISG Weirton. In April of 2005, ISG Weirton merged with Park Acquisition Corporation…a wholly owned subsidiary of Mittal Steel Company N. V., creating Mittal Steel USA, ArcelorMittal.

On February 9, 2009, Judy had gone to Wal Mart. Thurston was getting ready for work when he noticed a little nausea and began profusely sweating. Thurston asked his daughter, Victoria, who was staying with them at the time to drive him to the emergency room at the Weirton Medical Center. Thurston had a setback; he had thrown a blood clot that was blocking what they call the widow maker. Victoria called Judy, who came immediately, and a cardiologist was called. The doctor went in with a catheter, dissolved the blood clot, and put in a stint. Thurston was awake during the procedure. The doctor pointed at the monitor and told Thurston, "This is what it looked like before, showing the blockage. This is what it looks like now with the stint."

Thurston was amazed that he could be awake and more especially seeing it on the monitor. As he looked around the room, he could see two men with a cart. Actually, they were waiting in anticipation to life flight him to Presbyterian Hospital in Pittsburgh, Pennsylvania, if needed.

"Thank God the doctor lived close," replied Judy, sitting at Thurston's bedside in the coronary care unit, holding back tears.

"For sure, he saved my life. I'm lucky to be alive."

The heart attack weakened Thurston's heart, and in April that same year, he had a pacemaker and defibrillator inserted. Thurston was off work for six and a half months.

On November 17, 2010, Thurston received a strange call from a gentleman who claimed he was from some kind of coalition and said he needed to talk to him immediately. He said it was confidential, and he needed to meet with Thurston, personally.

"Well, let me say this, I don't know who you are, and until you tell me what this is all about, I'm not meeting you anywhere."

"It's concerning your grandson, Riley Van Lorne, it is urgent that I talk with you. My full name is Benjamin Franklin Daiquiri. I am affiliated with a worldwide coalition in London, England, engulfing a great number of people. We have been collecting information for many years pertaining to the Great War. We fill that your grandson is a very important part of our mission and the future. I don't know if you are a drinking man, but I would greatly appreciate meeting over dinner and a drink, as gentlemen," replied the stranger, hoping that Thurston would accept.

"Since it is about my grandson, I will meet with you. When and where?" asked Thurston, only because Benjamin had a deep English accent that Thurston recognized. He called Judy to alert her that he would be late, and that he was meeting an English gentleman for dinner.

After meeting and shaking hands, Benjamin Daiquiri and Thurston were in an uneasy, watchful peace with each other. They sat now at the hotel bar on the outskirts of Pittsburgh at Station Square. The place was constructed of shiny plastic, expensive furniture, and indirect lighting. A cute waitress, whose largest item was a revealing, low-cut dress, who industriously replenished drinks when they got low, smiling at them, working for a big tip. Benjamin was an attorney from London, England.

"Are you two going to eat, Daiq, or were you getting a table?" asked the waitress. She stretched across the bar to put a new designer napkin under Benjamin's drink.

"Did you want to get a table, Thurston, or are you good here?"

"I'm liking the scenery here. What did she call you?" asked Thurston, chuckling.

"I'm sorry, Thurston," replied Benjamin, sort of embarrassed. "That's what people call me, like Shaq O'neal. They call me Daiq, short for Daiquiri, my last name."

"No problem, Daiq, but we should get a table and keep this confidential. How do you see it?"

"That's how I'm seeing it, let's move," said Daiq, leaving a sizable tip for the waitress, receiving and returning a huge smile.

Another beautiful waitress appeared and took their orders.

"I was unaware that you practiced law, Daiq, I'm impressed."

"Not a big thing in England, Thurston. There are a couple of reasons that I ask you here. By the way, I am acting for a collective steering committee and a small part of the coalition. I'm not acting on my own. We know that you are extremely familiar with the power plant in Stockton, Pennsylvania, being the past vice president. That is your connection. We found some interesting and important writings about your grandson. I'll call him Zeppy Riley. That is his connection. I am in direct contact with the president of the United States. We are all sworn to secrecy. Albert Fu Fu [real name Al Chan Fugi] is being observed daily by us and the FBI, the little bug rat."

The waitress returned with the food and kindly asked if there was anything else. Daiq politely ordered another drink and said that was all.

"You called him a bug rat. What does that mean?" asked Thurston, wondering if this meeting was a mistake.

"It means he's wacky, his elevator doesn't go to the top floor. He is educated much higher than his intelligence. Getting rid of him is like burning down your house to get rid of a rat—it's difficult. He has just received papers that his divorce is settled. In a few weeks, the retiring, wife-beating psycho that the FBI is after for conspiracy and terroristic actions will take off into the islands. They will never find him. That's where you come into the picture."

"I can't believe that same 'bug rat' tried to bust my son-in-law for terrorism and conspiracy."

"The president certainly knows everything about your son-in-law, and we appreciate what he and his friends were trying to accomplish in Stockton, Pennsylvania. Everything is brought to the president concerning national security. The entire West Wing of the White House was completely rebuilt after 911, updated with all new technologies and miles of cable. It's called the situation room where the president and all involved can engage face-to-face to all the nations and kingdoms of the world. Telephones are not used for secret negotiations, strictly teletype, so that there are no misconstrued conversations. The White House was completely remodeled in President Truman's time to safeguard the president. The interior was completely gutted and rebuilt with steel and concrete to protect from nuclear attack. Special polymers are now used in the doors and windows that can stop all projectiles that can be fired at the White House. It is completely sealed and checked daily against radiation. Personal security for the president remains secret and always will be. The president…can be secretly removed from the White House."

"Amazing, now what is my part in all this, Daiq," asked Thurston, becoming very interested and very curious about the connection of an English attorney and the president of the United States.

"Before I get into your part, I have to let you know about the Prince of Wales and your grandson," Daiq began as he ordered another drink.

CHAPTER 25

Cathy was messing with little Lola and decided she needed to call Victoria to get the real story on their dad. Sometimes dads say everything good…so she punched in Vicky's number on her cell and wouldn't you know it, she got her phone mail. *Do people spend their lives on the phone?* she thought. Vicky came on the line, picking up the call waiting and said, "Hello, Vicky here."

"Hello, can you talk? This is Cathy."

"Yeah, wait, let me get Mom off the line," answered Vicky, clicking off, then back on.

"Okay, what's happening with you and the new princess? I love that name Sahara Lola, it's unique."

"Well, we decided to call her Lola. Sounds like a good princess name. I can't believe she's three already. You have now moved to number three in the princess list, Vicky. Mom and dad just adore this little girl. She's beautiful and looks just like me, stickum up hair and all. She's cute. Anna was number one until Lola came. Lola is now, unconditionally, and probably forever, number one princess."

"Hope she grows up to be as intelligent as Aunt Vicky, that's me and Rie Guy, of course," spouted Vicky, with a slight touch of snootiness.

"She will surpass all of you, including Dad. How do you see him doing, after being knocked down with that blood clot to the widow maker and developing a heart condition? You and Mom are supposed to be watching him."

"I can't see too much change in his personality. Two good things happened: he quit smoking and he stopped drinking so much beer. That's a worry off Mom, and he looks real healthy. You know I'm living at Chestnut Ridge in Robinson Township now, near Pittsburgh. I'm working in Carnegie at the elementary school. It's close to my apartment, and I found a good place to get my BMW worked on. It's called Foreign Fix. Get it."

"Yes, I get it, you spoiled brat, some day I wish to be as rich as you, smarty," yelled Cathy, thinking that she and Jon are "moving on up, to the east side" themselves, as the Jefferson's song goes. Jon finally has a good-paying steady job and contributing to the budget. Life is good.

"Florida was made for you two," exclaimed Vicky. "Mom and Dad are coming to see you at the end of November, so I will talk to you later. Bye."

"Bye," said Cathy, giving Lola a hug and a kiss.

Jon waited until Cathy got off the phone and asked, "How many instruments is Rie Guy going to play. Did you see his room? There is a complete set of drums, two guitars, amplifier, a keyboard, a saxophone, and what about all those hand noisemakers?"

"Jon, he actually plays that entire group of instruments and choreographs them together. He has songs and music on YouTube, and he is putting together a garage band. *He is a musician of destiny!*"

Jon went over to Rie Guy's room. He was sitting there as if in deep thought. "What's up, buddy? You look like you lost your best girlfriend."

"Maybe you're right, Dad, it's like letting go of a helium-filled balloon. It goes away pretty quick."

"That is deep. How you doing with the Radiohead band? You still like them? They are from the seventies."

"They're okay. I'm sort of writing and playing on my own now. You know what I mean."

"Yeah, I know what you mean…writing, playing, and choreographing music at age twelve. Fuge was right, you are something different. How do you like your room?" asked Jon, not believing what he's hearing from his son, *the musician of destiny!*

"My room, my instruments of pure awesomeness, a hardcore destiny lied before a musician, for he shall create the hardcore melodic sounds of destruction upon the earth by using the one they call the guitar, the mighty six strings of awesomeness, the main tool of rock 'n roll… and my closet too…"

Rie Guy was quoting from someone or from outer space. Jon didn't know. *God has sent us a magnificent gift. I hope we can appreciate it enough*, Jon thought. He turned away and returned to where Cathy was messing with the computer. Life is good.

CHAPTER 26

"The Prince of Wales has been proclaimed to be the 'savior of the world,' continued Daiq. "The Prince of Wales's intention is to be seen as the defender of faiths… to prevent the death of millions. I am appalled by that statement. To truly understand the prince, you know it is important to understand his father, the Duke of Edinburgh. The Duke of Edinburgh was a Eugenicist who wanted to reduce the population of this earth from a current level of 6 billion human bodies to much less than 1 billion within the next two generations. Do you believe that bloody crap? To somewhat quote the unrealistic Duke of freaking Edinburgh, 'In the event that I am reincarnated, I would like to return as a deadly virus, in order to eliminate people to solve the overpopulation.' The Prince of Wales is to be immortalized in bronze as a muscular, winged god dressed in nothing more than a loincloth in Brazil. Although the prince is destined to become defender of the faiths if he becomes King of England, the inscriptions will honor him as the savior of the world. Bullcrap! This designation just reeks of the title antichrist! That is a lot of poppycock, a bunch of freaking bullshit in American terms. The mighty demonic spirit of lying and deception will surely fail at the time it appears."

"I've never heard of anything like that about the prince," responded Thurston, not believing what he was hearing.

"I agree, Thurston. England abounds with folklore in all forms from such obvious manifestations of traditional Robin Hood tales to realistic contemporary legends and facets of cryptozoology. We now have the Prince of Wales as the 'savior of the world.' Some stories have been traced back to there roots while the origin of others are certainly disputed. That brings me to your grandson, Zeppy Riley, a terrific piece of folklore or legend that we have come in touch with and truly believe. We have traced history back to the time of King Henry VIII and his wife Catherine of Aragon whom he was married to for twenty-four years, making her the queen of England. We also traced you, Thurston, and your daughter Catherine back to a very stately family that began in Chester, Cheshire, England. John Blackshaw, of Chester, England, is a direct descendant of your daughter Catherine's great-great-grandfather."

"What does that mean?" asked Thurston, not letting on that he had done his own research.

"It means that the last writing of Catherine of Aragon, the queen of England who was cast from the thrown into calamities because she was unable to produce a male heir to the throne. She acquired a new title in life as Dowager Princess of Wales. The letter was addressed to her beloved king and past husband and definitely connects to you and your daughter."

"How could that connect to my daughter and I?" asked Thurston, being closed mouth and devious.

"There were many other letters forgiving Henry for all his wrongdoings, but there is only one that mentioned the firstborn son of Catherine of Cheshire. Not too many people have seen this particular letter that identifies a future prince who shall share the powers of royalty and acquire mindful strengths beyond those of any worldly being, a savior of mankind and refers to Sir Zep. Now, Thurston, I will guarantee you that the intended prince in the letter is not the Prince of Wales. Our conclusion is that we are putting all our apples in one basket. We are staying with your grandson, and that any further conversation that goes along with this, Zeppy Riley will be the code word and password. Do you understand? No one must know about this. You can include your wife, Catherine and her husband."

"Yes, and I want to apologize for playing dumb about the letter. I have certainly ventured into the letter, which I searched long and hard on the Internet and found everything that you have mentioned. I put all the pieces together and came up with the same conclusion. I know all about the chain of firstborn children. We can talk about that later. My wife Judy and I decided not to say anything to my daughter and her husband. She says we will just wait and watch."

"All right, that is absolutely great," replied Daiq. "I suppose you want to know about your part in all of this, don't you?"

"Yes, that would certainly help," said Thurston, very anxious about what Daiq was going to say.

"First, the FBI will intercept Albert Fu Fu before he can depart for the islands, with warrants for his arrest for conspiracy, and proceed to prosecute him for his crimes. We have talked to the Board of Directors at the Stockton Nuclear Power Plant and the new president of the United States. We all agree that you, Thurston, will be rehired at the power plant as the temporary CEO with total back pay from the time of your retirement—and a huge retirement. You, with the help of some of our programmed people, will train John Howard for the CEO position. You will be informed of our future plans for the power plant. Two million dollars will be put up in escrow until Riley Giuseppe Van Lorne is ready for higher education, and he will have complete guidance all through his studies. He will also be set up at Harvard University in Cambridge, Massachusetts, with everything he will ever need.

"He will have military training throughout his education. We understand his grandfather attended Harvard, and he will be a good reference."

Harvard University is an American Ivy League Research University located in Cambridge, Massachusetts, United States, established in 1636 by the Massachusetts legislature. Harvard is the oldest institution of higher education in the United States. Harvard's history, influence, and wealth have made it one of the most prestigious universities in the world.

"His continuing education will be at Oxford University or Cambridge University, closer to my home in London, England, United Kingdom."

The University of Oxford is a university located in Oxford, England, United Kingdom. It is the oldest university in the English-speaking world, and the second oldest surviving university in the world.

The University of Cambridge is a university located in Cambridge, England, United Kingdom. It is the second oldest university in the English-speaking world, and the fourth oldest surviving university in the world.

"Are you seeing it, Thurston? That should cover the parts of Queen Catherine's letter to King Henry VIII that refers to the firstborn son of Catherine Michelle Van Lorne of Bartow, Florida, whom we have declared Catherine of Cheshire because of ancestry. It says that he shall share the powers of royalty and acquire mind strengths beyond worldly beings. We don't look on Zeppy Riley as an antichrist. We see him as one who will change history and stop the inevitable war that would end mankind by nuclear nonproliferation and a worldwide disarmament movement."

"I am stunned," said Thurston, trying to collectively put together everything that just transpired. "I have to have some time to put this all together."

"I will give you two weeks to think it over. You must remember that this is top secret. You can call me any time to refresh anything that we have talked about. Here is my business card. The code word is Zeppy Riley, and we must meet if you call. We can't have any conversation on the phone. I will set up a place for us to meet. If you don't call within the two weeks, I will call you. This has been a pleasure, Thurston. I hope that you will accept the offer. This isn't a dream."

"It's a win-win proposition," exclaimed Thurston. "How could I refuse?"

"Your biggest issue is keeping all of this a secret from Riley. He is going to be very curious where everything is coming from. I imagine you can tell him that his fairy godmother came through with some huge money. The kids in England all believe in elves and sprites."

They shook hands and said good-bye.

CHAPTER 27

Driving home from Pittsburgh at eleven o'clock at night wasn't bad. The traffic was pretty quiet. Thurston had about one hundred things going though his head. He thought about telling Judy that he had dinner at Station Square in Pittsburgh with an English gentleman named Benjamin Franklin Daiquiri, a lawyer from London, England, United Kingdom—yeah, right.

"The codeword is Zeppy Riley and we are sworn to utmost secrecy," muttered Thurston as he gave Judy a peck on the cheek. "I met with an English lawyer from London, England, who blew my mind. That's why I'm so late."

"I'm picturing you out with your drunken friends again. You are always telling me stories. Remember the time when you came traipsing in at two o'clock. You told me that a huge airline jet had made a force landing on the highway and that all the little cars could get under the wing, but our car just wouldn't fit. I've heard them all. They must have run out of brains when you got there, and they gave you that nice wooden one instead."

"Judy, I am serious, do you remember when I did all that digging on the Internet looking for the letter that Catherine, the outcast queen of England had written to King Henry VIII. There is a coalition in England that had come up with the same conclusions as I did about Rie Guy. This lawyer's name is Benjamin Franklin Daiquiri. He is apparently a big part of the coalition and deals directly with our president in the United States. He got in contact with me by calling my office. We met and he explained everything."

"I won't insult your intelligence by suggesting that you really believe what you just said. Sometimes I think you carry things a bit too far. We need to give that a rest and go to bed," suggested Judy as she reached to turn off the living room light and retire to the bedroom.

"Look, he gave me his business card. I can call him at any time using the code word that I told you, and he will meet me. He is staying in the Pittsburgh area for two weeks, until I think it over about Rie Guy. He is an absolute true believer in Rie Guy as a savior of mankind. They are putting huge money in escrow for his education and military training to make it all happen. This is real, Judy, and we can only tell Catherine and Jon, no one else. It is top-secret, and Rie Guy must never know. It's like what Frederick Douglass, an abolitionist, once quoted, 'It's easier to build strong children than to repair broken men.' That's what we're talking about. Zeppy Riley has to be built."

"You scare me when you start quoting people. I see the card and it does say that Benjamin Franklin Daiquiri is a lawyer from London. And he deals with our president, Thurston. What? You believe this bullshit? You can't believe this bullshit? Are you always this stupid or are you making a special effort today?"

"There's more, Judy, Albert Fu Fu is being watched at the nuclear power plant in Stockton, Pennsylvania, by the coalition and the Federal Bureau of Investigation for the United States for conspiracy. He will be taken into custody in two or three weeks. They want me to take over as chief executive officer for an unknown length of time to train John Howard for that position. Their will be a lot of changes in the process. It has passed through the board of directors and the president of the United States, who still remembers Jon. They are giving me back pay from the time of my retirement from the power plant, a new salary as chief executive officer, and a huge pension. Now who's stupid?"

"For real, Thurston, I can't believe it. Is it true? Come on. I couldn't believe you until you said about the CEO position. You wouldn't kid about that. If this is all true, I am ecstatic. Please say it's all true or pinch me to see if I'm dreaming."

"You aren't dreaming. It's for real. I have to give him an answer within the two weeks. I'll tell you all about it. I can't think of anything but yes, can you, Judy?"

"As we said before, Thurston, we'll have to wait and watch."

"We'll have to delay our trip to Florida we were planning, for a couple of weeks. I can't wait to tell Cathy and Jon about everything, we can't do it on the phone."

"I guess you weren't a waste of good sperm, after all, Thurston."

"Yeah, right, love you and good night."

"Good night."

CHAPTER 28

Thurston and Judy thought it over and talked it over for more than a week. Thurston decided to call and meet with Benjamin Franklin Daiquiri to let him know that he is going along with the plan, also to see if the plan was nothing but a scam or not. He dialed Daiq's number and hoped that there would be an answer.

"Hello, Thurston, Zeppy Riley. I hope you have put all your doubts to bed, and we can continue with what we're going to accomplish. I am sure it will be a positive answer when we meet at the Holiday Inn. We'll talk then."

"Good evening, Daiq, as I said before, when opportunity knocks, you have to answer or be a fool the rest of your life. How do you see it, Daiq?"

"You've convinced me. Now, in order to kick all of this off, I have to show you a contract that you must sign. You have to abide by the contract or the deal is off. It states that you will go along with all the wishes of the coalition and the president of the United States. As you see, there are many official authorized signatures. We believe that your grandson is the answer that we are looking for. He must be molded and structured to meet our desires. We know that he has the strength, the ability, and the intelligence that is needed for this structuring. He will be educated in top fashion and militarily trained to hurdle all obstacles that might present themselves. In the almost forty years in the nuclear age, de facto nuclear proliferation has led to eight nations definitely having nuclear weapons, the US, Russia, England, France, China, India, Pakistan, and Israel, which has yet to publicly admitted it. I have no idea about that. The Nuclear Nonproliferation Treaty was signed on July 1968 and entered into force on March 1970. Central to the treaty is the concession of the non-nuclear weapons states to refrain from acquiring nuclear weapons, and in exchange, the nuclear weapons states to make progress on nuclear disarmament and provide unrestricted access to nuclear energy for nonmilitary uses. You following, Thurston? Freaking Cuba, India, Israel, and Pakistan have refused to sign. What we are looking for with Zeppy Riley is to lay the cornerstones for global disarmament of all nuclear weapons. Are you staying with me so far, Thurston?"

"Not an easy task," answered Thurston. "My son-in-law Jon and I have pretty much ventured into that as an impossible happening, but I will definitely do as I am told. What about the Stockton Nuclear Power Plant?"

"That will be your baby. We have special plans for you, as CEO of the plant, that has to be glued together by John Howard and yourself. We also have done some research on people, and we fill that a nuclear expert, Hoy Lee Chong Grant, will be your chief operating officer to put all this together. He worked at the power plant previously. Did you know him?"

"My God, he was the lifeblood of the plant when I was vice president. He is the smartest man that I have run into in my entire career. He is definitely a God-send, and certainly a team player. He is an excellent choice."

"You read the contract over thoroughly, sign it, and we will meet again in two days. Contact me, and I will set up a place. We need to meet at different places each time so that no one gets suspicious. Remember, the code word is Zeppy Riley."

"Gotcha," said Thurston, exhausted from absorbing the information from the meeting.

They said their good-byes and Thurston was on his way home again. He could hardly wait to tell Judy about Hoy Lee Chong and all that had happened. It was a highly improbable dream.

Thurston and Daiq met two days later in Robinson Township, near Pittsburgh, at a restaurant and bar called Ditka's. Ditka's in Robinson is the third restaurant location of Super Bowl–winning Aliquippa, Pennsylvania, native Mike Ditka.

Michael Keller Ditka was a former NFL player, Chicago Bears, who participated in two Chicago Bears' championships, in 1963 and as head coach in 1985. He was also a television sports commentator.

Thurston had brought along the signed contract and Daiq had met him at the door, shook hands, and they entered. Daiq had already had a drink and was about to order another and ask Thurston if he wanted a drink. Thurston said he would have a light beer.

"This place is great, Thurston, I've been here twice and the food is fantastic, especially the steak. The Kansas

City strip had a texture of filet but the flavor of a robust, chewy strip, and it was perfectly cooked from edge to bone. In addition, the salads and sides are excellent but relatively light, which limits the typical steakhouse bloat. Being from England, I understand that word. I make the reservation online, and they are anxiously seating you as soon as you arrive. Then you have the run of the place. I mean you do what you want. Get up, walk around."

"I can see that you like your food and drink," remarked Thurston.

"When you are on the road a lot, like me, you learn to enjoy restaurants. I see you brought the contract. Not a lot to it, is there?"

"Ten pages isn't bad, really, I have seen larger ones."

"We're talking about a lot of cash in this transaction, we have to protect ourselves," replied Daiq, swooshing his drink around.

The waitress arrived with menus, and after replenishing their drinks, they ordered from the menu.

"Okay, Thurston, you and I and Hoy Lee Chong will meet at the Stockton Nuclear Power Plant after the holidays, on the third of January. John Howard is in charge as acting CEO until then. There is no reason to go over the details of the plan until we all meet. There will be eight of us when we meet, and we want everyone on the same page, two from the coalition and two from the United States government, John, Chong, you, and I. No problem. Now we can enjoy our meals."

"When do I contact you?" asked Thurston.

"On January 2 at noon, I will be expecting your call. Leave January 3 open on your calendar. Don't forget the code, Zeppy Riley."

"One more thing I wish to do after we get everything in place. I am going to interview Zeppy Riley as a reporter from the *Rolling Stone* magazine. I will have a cameraman with me, one of our people, so that we can observe his actions and his reactions. View his character. My British accent will enhance him, and he will be sooooo excited. We will set up the interview through you, Thurston. I have been affiliated with the *Rolling Stone* magazine for quite a while. I did some music and some gigs with a small band at Chancellors University. Chancellors University was truly spread out all over our capital of London, United Kingdom, as were most London-based colleges. Chancellors dated back to the sixteenth century. It was founded by King Henry VIII Chancellor, Cardinal Wolsey. Music was my friend. Music was my life. I attended a venue concert on an invitation by a classmate of mine at Chancellors, who was a reporter for *Rolling Stone* magazine. It was at Half Moon Putney, in Putney, London, which is one of London's longest-running and most respected live music venues. Since the early 1960s, some of the biggest names in the music world performed there, including the Rolling Stones, The Who, and U2. Backstage I interviewed one of the up-and-coming rock groups and did a complete write-up. My friend ran the interview for the *Rolling Stone* magazine, and overnight, that group became rock and roll superstars. Somehow the editors of the magazine found out that it was me that did the write-up. They paid me and said they would accept copies of any interview I wrote and possibly publish. I will turn in a copy of my interview of Zeppy Riley and see where it goes."

"This is beyond belief. My wife and daughter will be totally out of sorts about this, but elated. You also let me know when you want the interview," replied Thurston, totally shocked and impressed with Benjamin Franklin Daiquiri. "I will call you January 2, twelve o'clock, at noon."

CHAPTER 29

Thurston and Judith had booked a flight to Orlando, Florida, rented a vehicle from Hertz at the Orlando Airport, and were driving to the Pittsburgh International Airport. It was the third of December 2010. Thurston was busting at the seams, anticipating telling his daughter and Jon what all had transacted.

"What was wrong with that Albert Fu Fu? Was he on drugs or what? He had it perfectly made and blew it," asked Judy as she brushed back her hair.

"A known wife-beater and no one would know how far he got conspiring with those terrorists. There is a fine line between psychic and psycho when listening to the voices in your head," quoted Thurston. "He had just received the wrong messages."

"Did you just make that up? I don't know what makes you so dumb, but it really works. You know I don't like those sayings. Are you sure you are going to be safe as CEO of a nuclear power plant, Thurston?"

"I feel completely safe, besides, Hoy Lee Chong will be there, and he's always got my back. I think I would have been a little leery or nervous if they wouldn't have put him in the equation as chief operating officer. His father actually trained him with all modern military weapons, including assault weapons. I have a lot of trust and admiration in Chong. No fear. He will forever protect me."

"Don't let that mind of yours wander…it's too small to be let out on its own. You will have total security at the power plant. Remember how Albert Fu Fu installed security entry codes in his office and the conference rooms. If I were you, I would double the security officers there, not knowing what went on when Albert was in charge."

"Albert Einstein once said, 'Anyone who has never made a mistake has never tried anything new.' I'm trying something new, and it may be a mistake. Who knows?"

"We'll just have to wait and watch, won't we, Thurston?"

After checking in at the airport, entering and exiting the check point, they went on the tram to their concourse and boarded the plane. When they landed in Orlando, Florida, they picked up their luggage and acquired their rental car. They left the Orlando airport and traversed to Interstate Route 4, heading for Bartow, Florida. They got a room at the Holliday Inn Express in Bartow, making the trip more like a vacation. When they arrived at Washingtonia Court, the Van Lornes, Jon, Cathy, Rie Guy, Lola, and their five cats were excitedly waiting. They all hugged; Rie Guy always liked group hugs, saves time he would say. Lola was the entertaining princess as always and Rie Guy was anxious to show Mimi and Fuge all of his musical equipments. They rested for a little while and met on the outside carport that had nice comfortable furniture. The kids were inside entertaining themselves. Judy and Thurston told Jon and Cathy about all that had transacted with Benjamin Franklin Daiquiri, the attorney from London, England, who was with a coalition there and who dealt in person with the president of the United States. Thurston told Jon that they wanted him back at the power plant as CEO and Hoy Lee Chong as the chief operating officer. He told him about Albert Fu Fu being busted as a conspirator with terrorists.

"He's the sucker that wanted to bust the Ratt Pack for that same exact thing," exclaimed Jon, lighting up a cigarette. "What a creep, I never liked him, too sneaky."

"Tell them about Rie Guy and about Queen Catherine. Tell them about the Rolling Stone interview and Rie Guy's future," yelled Judy, so excited that she was about to have a breakdown.

Thurston went on to explain the whole thing, which took about an hour. Jon and Cathy sat there with their mouths gaping open in disbelief, but it was all real and about to happen. Jon also had to sign a contract.

"One thing," said Thurston, getting a really serious look on his face. "Rie Guy must never know the answers to these questions. Who set up all this education and training? Why are they doing all this? Where is the money coming from? We'll just say that Mimi and Fuge came into some money. Cathy, you are the one who has to prepare him. He will have to keep up a good grade point average and take the right courses. You are the one that is most familiar with the curriculum he will need. Enough said. Love you, guys. Now, let's go get something to eat. I like that Ruby Tuesdays."

"I'm so excited, Dad," replied Cathy, finding it hard to breath.

Judy and Thurston spent the week in Bartow, returned the vehicle, and caught their flight home from the Orlando international Airport.

"When did you say your meeting is at the power plant, Thurston? By the way, you did a terrific job explaining everything to Cathy and Jon. I'm proud of you."

"We will meet on January 3. I have to call Daiq on the second, at noon, to confirm the meeting. You and I will probably stay a couple of days at the Holiday Inn in Stockton. Ben Franklin once said, I mean the real Ben Franklin, not Daiq, 'Well done is better than well said.' I will be glad when this meeting is well done," replied Thurston.

"Will you stop quoting people? I'm visualizing you with duct tape over your mouth. Your lips are moving, but all I hear is 'blah, blah, blah.'"

"An injury is much sooner forgotten than an insult."

"I'm going to give you an injury if you don't stop it. You should have an 'out of order' sign on your forehead," laughed Judy, winking at Thurston.

CHAPTER 30

On January 3, 2011, a meeting at the Stockton, Pennsylvania, Nuclear Power Plant was about to begin at 9:00 am. Attending the meeting were two representatives from the United States government, Richard Vixen, and Ronald Reason; both were obviously packing heat. Two representatives from the London coalition were Charles James Scott and Annabelle Miller who could have possibly been packing heat. Hoy Lee Chong Grant, who also had a license to carry, John Howard who wouldn't know what to do with a gun, Daiq and Thurston.

Richard vixen was tall and slender but built like a wedge. He had a stone-cold face that could only be matched at a Texas hold'em poker game. His eyes seemed to shift in every direction as if he were suspicious of everything around him. He could have been a security guard for the president.

Ronald Reason was a little heavier but about the same height. He looked about six-foot-two-inches tall and possibly weighed two hundred and fifty pounds. He had a terminal stare that felt as if he was punching holes into people. Both he and Mr. Vixen certainly got your attention.

Charles James Scott, who preferred to be called Charley, around forty years old, was a more pleasant-looking man. He dressed in designer clothing and wore a flat toilet seat hat. He had a British accent that matched Daiq's almost perfectly. He seemed eager to get started with the meeting.

Annabelle Miller was a total knockout of about thirty-five years old. She had a black belt in Tae Kwon Do and what looked like a strong, healthy body. She was five-foot-eight and seemed to look stronger than most men. She had a beautiful smile and a top model's face. She was dressed in blue jeans and a sweatshirt. She was all business.

Daiq started by introducing everyone, then he began explaining. "I'm not going to pull any punches about what we are doing here, and I want everyone on the same page. We feel there were negotiations with conspirators from a Muslim or Oriental country and members of the work force in this plant. Albert Fu Fu has been taken into custody, but he isn't talking. My greatest fear is that there may be more conspirators that we have not been identified. The government agents that the president has graciously supplied, Mr. Vixen and Mr. Reason, have been trained as high intelligence weapons experts who will flush out these conspirators if they exist in the plant. Mr. Beltow who was once vice president for many years will be the new chief executive officer. Hoy Lee Chong Grant will be the new chief operating officer. Eventually, John Howard will take over the top spot, and Mr. Grant will remain as COO. Our mission is to deter whatever plans have been laid out to confiscate the modules that we hold in what they call the Bunker. We can not bow down to these terrorists, and we can't take the chance of moving the modules because they may be watching, and it would make the modules an easy target. Everyone in this room has taken an oath to keep the operations running here because it serves a big portion of Pennsylvania with energy. I will stay in constant contact with Thurston, and we are hoping that this will all go away as peaceably as possible. Everyone is assigned an area to watch, and we have enhanced the security by ten armed watchman. Are there any questions?"

"Are we all being issued weapons?" asked John Howard with wide eyes.

"No, only people who are licensed to carry. All others must trust and stand behind them. Also no one in the plant can know why this operation is happening. It is business as usual."

"Can we leave the plant for lunch or any other needs?" asked Annabelle, pulling her long hair into a ponytail.

"You can leave one or two at a time. You must sign out and sign back in at the gate," replied Daiq, wondering why Annabelle Smith has chosen this as an occupation.

"How long can we expect to be here?" asked Richard Vixen.

"It will time itself. We can't predict at this point. Okay, let's wrap this up. Everyone starts three days from now. Everyone will have a couple days off a week. We can make a schedule to suit everyone's needs. Good-bye and I will be in touch."

It was Monday, January 6; everyone had reported at the power plant as planned. Thurston wanted everyone to meet in the smaller conference room connected to his office. Everyone was given the codes for the security locks. Thurston had made out a weekly schedule, which met everyone's needs. No one needed any further instructions on what to do.

"My wife Judith's favorite expression is that we will have to wait and watch, and basically, that is what we are assigned to do here. I will not be placed on any schedule, but I expect to be here as much as I possibly can. I have rented a home in Stockton, near the plant. For at least two weeks, I will not take a day off. Hoy Lee Chong Grant has rented a home close to me, and we will probably spend a lot of time together, along with John Howard."

"I, for one, am expecting to do the same thing," replied Annabelle. "I will spend most of my time in and around the plant."

"Ditto," said Rich Vixon and Ron Reason almost simultaneously.

"We're planning on hanging around a good bit of the time," said Ron, looking proud and crossing his arms. "We have rented apartments, and we are bringing our wives to spend time here also."

"Well, that makes it unanimous. We will all be hanging around most of our time here," uttered Charley, smiling and wiping his forehead.

"Okay," spouted Thurston. "We are all on a base salary, so their will be no overtime. Thanks for your loyalty."

Thurston closed the meeting, and they were all on there way out. Annabelle asked Thurston if he minded if she spent her time around John, Chong, and himself, sort of for their protection. Thurston said he would appreciate that and that he had full trust in her. She was carrying a loaded weapon on her hip and a complete utility belt, with mace, cuffs, and a long police club.

"I'm here as your personal security," Annabelle informed him.

As the months passed, there wasn't much happening at the power plant, and things were easing up. It remained business as usual. Thurston and Judith had shared a few meals with Charley and Annabelle, Chong, and John. They all became good friends. Daiq kept in contact with Thurston and was thankful that there were no problems. He told Thurston that he was getting anxious to interview his grandson, and if everything stayed calm, they would fly to Florida for a couple of weeks. Daiq would interview Rie Guy, and he would do a complete write-up for *Rolling Stone* magazine in San Francisco, California. That should give us a good look at his character, his thoughts, and how he basically carries himself.

"I'm thinking about the first of May, that weekend, we will have to take a good look at those dates, all right, and you know that I will keep in close touch. Bye."

"Sounds good to me," said Thurston, thinking it would be good to get away for a couple of days. "You know Judy will have to come along."

"I was counting on that, Thurston. Later, mate."

Thurston said good-bye.

CHAPTER 31

Daiq had rented a private jet that would fly out of the executive section of Pittsburgh International Airport at 9:40 am on April 30, bound for Orlando Executive Airport, located only three miles from the business and financial center in central Florida. Orlando Executive Airport, operated by The Greater Orlando Aviation Authority, has a convenient access to all of Orlando's major highways. Daiq loved this airport.

"In addition," smiled Daiq. "The door-to-door service makes the transition from air to ground transportation easy and effortless. A limo will be waiting that we will have full use for the five days that we are staying. First, Thurston and I and my camera man, John McHallyo, have packed our golf clubs so there will be a day of golfing at Lake Regions Golf and Yacht Club, where Jon was assistant pro, located in Winter Haven, Florida. Second, we will have a partial day interviewing Rie Guy, followed by a visit to a couple of water parks around the area. Third, we will stay overnight at the Caribbean Beach Resort at Disney World, in Lake Buena Vista, Florida, for two days. Finally we will return to the airport and fly back to Pittsburgh, Pennsylvania. The itinerary and reservations are already set up. The trip is being funded by me, not to worry."

"Why did I know that there would be golf involved?" spouted Judy, reaching for her seat belt in the small six-passenger-seat jet. "That had to be Thurston's idea. He was born without a brain, you know."

Daiq laughed and said, "Thurston doesn't stand a chance around you, Judy. You and Thurston are quite entertaining."

At the Lake Regions Golf Club, on May 1, Daiq, Jon, Thurston, and John McHallyo were preparing to hit their drives off the first tee.

"Thurston has told me so many things about you and Rie Guy, Jon, which I feel like I've known you forever. Are you still with the impression that something has to be done before all hell breaks loose in the entire world? Some country will eventually push the panic button. You think?"

"I've been fighting this battle my entire life, Daiq. I think Thurston said it right one time about trying to empty out an Olympic-size swimming pool with a teaspoon or about pulling on a string and there is just no end to it. As long as the United States has presence in the Middle East and they are tight allies with Israel, there is going to be trouble. Israel may be the first country to push that panic button, and naturally, the United States will be the place to suffer. We will be the target of many countries, and that is a fact. I believe that the Nuclear Non-Proliferation Treaty's existence is threatened by countries that refuse to sign the treaty who want to acquire nuclear weapons that destroy the progress of nuclear disarmament of the countries that have them."

"Well said," agreed Thurston as he bent over to tee up his ball.

"Hooray," replied Daiq. "Very few people know and understand that we are coming to the crossroads. That's why we at the coalition and some of the higher ups in the United States all feel we have to hold onto the predictions that pertain to Zeppy Riley to change the course of the avenue that we are traveling. It is a greater hope than some of the predictions of Nostradamus and World War Three and its relations to Bible prophecy. Zeppy Riley will be the answer."

"Okay, let's play golf, no more of that talk today," yelled John McHallyo as he grabbed one of the beers on his golf cart and popped it open.

"Yeah," they all responded.

Daiq was preparing everything for the interview and was telling Rie guy not to be nervous. John McHallyo would shoot a video of the whole thing.

"Just visualize that I am one of your friends asking you questions. The answers will come automatically. Okay, here we go."

"This is Benjamin Franklin Daiquiri. I am sitting with Riley Giuseppe Van Lorne who I feel is a pretty talented individual. Most relatives and his friends call him Rie or Rie Guy and I will stick with Rie Guy. Rie Guy self-taught himself all the instruments you see behind us in his room at his home in Bartow, Florida. Rie Guy writes his own music and choreographs himself playing all these instruments and singing his own lyrics on YouTube. We want to get to know him so I will ask him a few questions. By the way, Rie Guy also plays in a garage band as a guitarist and vocals with some of his friends. Hello, Rie Guy."

"Hello," responded Rie Guy.

"First, most of the girls want to know if you are married."

"I'm only thirteen. I will be fourteen, August 1."

"Good answer. Are you nervous about this interview?"

"Of course I'm not. I love your magazine."

"Where do you attend school?"

"Bartow High School, I also play in the school band, saxophone."

"What do you like about school?"

"Yeah …long weekends."

"What do you dislike about school?"

"Bullying in all schools"

"How would you suggest we stop all the bullying?"

"I had more than my share of bullying. My father enrolled me in the after-school pick-up program at the Tae Kwon Do Academy in Lakeland, Florida."

"Did they teach you to protect yourself?"

"Tae Kwon Do teaches more then physical fighting skills. It is a discipline that shows ways of enhancing our spirit and life by training our body and mind."

"What is funny to you, Rie Guy?"

"My cat!"

"Why is your cat funny?"

"My cat was sleeping on the snare of my drum set. I put a shirt over it to mute the sound, and apparently

Remy, my cat, found it comfortable. Lol, laugh out loud, which is going to be the cover of my band's album."

"What is serious, Rie Guy?"

"So much judgment…. We can't accept each other, we can't accept what others believe in, we can't accept each other's lifestyles, we can't accept what others think, and we can't accept how a person is because that is human nature apparently. It is human nature to be cruel and unforgiving, it is human nature to be horrible and merciless, it is the natural habitat, the savage bond, and the way of living for humans…. I guess I'm not human…"

"That was pretty deep, Rie Guy, did you hear that somewhere?"

"Just repeating something I learned, I guess."

"Who is most important to you?"

"Probably my mom."

"Why Mom?"

"Total support, she says our band is awesome."

"What is the band's response to that?"

"Thank you, Mrs. Van Loooooorne."

"What do you think of politics?"

"I have no interest in politics, and I don't like war."

"Good thinking, Rie Guy. Why do you like music?"

"Music is my life…the lyrics are my story.…"

"Explain music, Rie Guy."

"Music is a teenager's life, sometimes music is the only thing for teens when no one else can be there for them. Music is really the only thing that understands and gets to teens when no one else does."

"Wow, Rie Guy, that was great. Describe Rie Guy."

"I'm a mellow kind of guy, very laid back and chilled. I'm a musician and an artist. I have no religion, but I believe in God."

"I'm going to cut this off now, Rie. This has been a pleasure and very interesting. We hope we can make whatever dreams you have come true. One more question, what is your most precious dream?"

"Be a rock star!" replied Rie Guy, throwing his arms out to his sides.

"Thank you, Rie Guy."

CHAPTER 32

Jon was trying to get hold of Thurston at the Holiday Inn Express. He couldn't believe what he was hearing on the television. They got Osama bin Laden. Thurston finally answered, and Jon couldn't spit it out fast enough.

"I hope you weren't busy. It's almost two o'clock. Do you have your television on? They got that sucker. They got bin Laden."

"We just came back from lunch with Daiq. He just returned from Rie Guy's interview and was very impressed with him. Let me get the television on. All of us are going to Disney this afternoon, you know. Lola's going to love this trip. Oh, I see, looks like the Navy Seals' got him. That's fantastic! He has been free too long. Daiq is here, he's seeing it also, thank God."

Osama bin Laden, the louse, the founder and head of the Islamist militant group Al-Qaeda, was apparently killed in Pakistan on May 2, 2011, shortly after 1:00 am local time by the Navy Seals of the United States Naval Special Warfare Development Group. The operation, codenamed Operation Neptune Spear, was executed in a CIA-led operation. After the raid, United States forces took Osama bin Laden to Afghanistan to identify his body. He was then buried at sea within twenty-four hours of his death.

"I don't think I've ever been so happy," shouted Jon. "Maybe now we can pull some troops out of Afghanistan. I know there is a lot more to do there, but I'm always hoping for the United States to clear out of that Middle East. Right, Thurston."

"Yeah," said Thurston. "We all feel the same about all that. Okay, Jon, get your kids ready. We'll be picking you, Cathy, and the kids up in the limo around four o'clock."

Jon was still thinking that if Al-Qaeda confirmed bin Laden's death, they will vow to avenge his death, especially after Jon had listened to the legal aspects of the killing, such as bin Laden not being taken alive despite being unarmed. *Oh well*, he thought, *time to go to see the Magic Kingdom at Lake Buena Vista.*

"We can hit one of the water parks today, and starting tomorrow, we will try to hit a couple of the theme parks, especially the Magic Kingdom for the kids. We'll try to see as much as we can because we have a full package of tickets for all of us and two full days to spend them," exclaimed Daiq.

The Walt Disney World Resort, commonly known as *Walt Disney World*, is the world's most-visited entertainment resort. It is strategically located in Lake Buena Vista, Florida, and covers 30,080 acres. The resort is owned and operated by The Walt Disney Company through its parks and resorts division. What a beautiful layout. It is the home of four theme parks, two water parks, five golf courses, and many other recreational and entertainment venues. The resort was the brainchild of Walt Disney in the sixties, intentionally supplementing Disneyland Park in Anaheim, California. Walt Disney died in 1966 before his original plans were completed. The resort opened in October 1971 with the Magic Kingdom as its only theme park, adding Epcot, Disney's Hollywood Studios, and Disney's Animal Kingdom later.

After two of the most fun-filled, tiring days that they all had spent in their entire lives, it was over. Lola and Rie Guy loved every minute of it. They were totally elated. The limo transported them back to Bartow, and the next day delivered Daiq, Thurston, Judy and John McHallyo back to the Orlando Executive Airport for their flight back to Pittsburgh. It took a full day for all of them to recover.

Thurston was back at the nuclear power plant, and Annabelle Miller was again right in has back pocket.

"Did you miss me, Annabelle?" asked Thurston. "Do you believe that I had six days without a shadow?"

"I'll remember that when someone comes in here, ready to tear off a piece of your ass. How's that sound? Mr. big shot," snarled Annabelle, looking at him with evil eyes.

"Just kidding, Annabelle, I appreciate you, honest," groaned Thurston.

"I'm just kidding, too, you big dummy. I totally love watching over you. You are such a wimp."

"I resemble that remark," Thurston muttered.

"You sure do."

"Have Rich Vixen and Ron Reason found any conspiring suspects since I've been gone?" asked Thurston, stretching out his arms.

"Everyone looks relatively clean. Albert must have been acting alone as far as we can see."

"The way I see it, winter's almost over, and I will enjoy the springtime collecting chief executive officer's salary. Can hardly beat that, can you?"

"No, you can't, boss," answered Annabelle, giving Thurston a bone-crushing hug. "Welcome back."

"Weren't you going to show me the escape route out of here in case of a terrorist attack or a complete meltdown? You were going to show me when we got back from Florida," asked Thurston.

"Yes, and this is a good time to show you, while no one else is around," replied Annabelle, pointing at the interior wall of his office. "Albert Fu Fu had this installed twelve years ago."

Annabelle walked over to the wall, reached for the upper right hand corner of the huge television screen, pulled a lever, and a small section of the wall popped open. She told Thurston that there was no electricity involved in case the power went out. It led to a steep stairway and descended to a long tunnel. There were rails running down the middle of the tunnel, and a small carlike module that ran on the rails and could hold six people. There were six sets of protective clothing complete with breathing apparatuses. This would have been the escape route that Albert would have used. She had explained that the six seats were reserved for Jill Walinski, his secretary, and his friend, Richard Harmin's daughter,

Charley, Chong, Thurston, herself, John Howard, and no one else. The tunnel was actually four miles long and was indestructible because of the thickness of the concrete. At the other end of the tunnel was an armored vehicle that can hold twenty to twenty-five people and can travel eighty miles per hour. It contained two battery packs so that there is no failure at start up. The vehicle was completely air-tight with a filtering system that will deter any radiation within the interior. Video cameras were placed throughout the power plant and could be seen on the monitors in Jill's office and the security office. Security would be aware of everything in the plant by keeping an eye on the monitors. Security had direct contact with local authorities, the International Atomic Energy Authority, police, fire, and the National Guard.

"You're as snug as a bug in a rug, Thurston. You have no fear because you have me as your shadow and Jill to take care of your paper work," stated Annabelle after taking Thurston on a complete tour of the escape routes.

"I am impressed. My life is actually in your hands, Annabelle. You and Charley are the ones that are keeping this place running. Daiq certainly knew what he was doing when he placed you and Charley here. Charley is the greatest organizer I have ever come in contact with."

"Charley and I are the best," replied Annabelle. "We have worked together a long time at the coalition in London. Daiq has always depended on us for years. There is no one in this world today that could compare to Daiq. He has always been a solid, strong leader who has never been married, and it is a great mystery how he became so wealthy. It is endless. It is almost as if he was sent as a guardian angel, who knows? I do know one thing. He has a lot of faith in that grandson of yours. He believes that your Zeppy Riley, the name that he refers to, is sent straight from heaven also."

"I have to agree," said Thurston as he went over by the television and closed the opening to the secret passage. "You just can't tell that the opening is there—unbelievable. Anyhow, I have been amazed and proud of our Rie Guy because he has always been so brilliant, but now I have developed the same feeling about Daiq. They are two of a kind."

CHAPTER 33

Thurston was daydreaming while sitting at his desk at the power plant when Jill buzzed him and said that her father was on the phone. Thurston picked up, and Jill transferred Richard Harmin over.

"Thurston, old boy, Joe Cipra and I were just talking to Jon, your son-in-law, and he just knocked our socks off when he told us that you were now the CEO of the Stockton Nuclear Power Plant and that Hoy Lee Chong Grant is COO. How in the hell did you pull that off?"

"You know that I've always been a magician, Shank, and I could not handle this job if it weren't for Chong and a couple of British co-workers. Also, the president of the United States has given me two top agents from the government and a huge enhancement of security. I don't know if you heard or read about our illustrious Albert Fu Fu, the past CEO, who got busted for conspiring secretly with another country. It was in all the newspapers."

"Yeah, we heard about that toad, couldn't have happened to a more deserving jerk. My daughter didn't even tell me about this, and she works right in your office."

"Really hasn't been that long. Besides, the president has only placed me here for a short period of time, John Howard eventually becomes the new chief executive officer. Chong will remain as chief operating officer when I leave."

"John Howard is afraid of his own shadow. How can they give him that top job? Hoy Lee Chong would be a better choice. Jon was telling us that you are hanging around with a multimillionaire who made a special trip to Bartow, Florida, to interview his son Riley, writing for a well-known magazine. Daiq, is that his name?"

"He's just a friend of mine, Tort Lawyer after pharmaceuticals, you know how those guys operate, corporate planes and all, milking the drug companies and keeping them straight. That interview may work out for Rie Guy someday. It can't hurt!"

"Jon told us about all the instruments your grandson can play and about his garage band. I remember he was going to call him Zeppy Riley," exclaimed Shank. "My two sons, Michael and John, seem to have pretty good heads on their shoulders. Wait, Joe Cipra wants to talk to you."

"Hi, Thurston, glad to hear you are doing well after your heart problems. I hope it continues. I still just have the one boy. Jon was telling us a little about his good buddy Judge Clydesdale. He seems to be doing all right in Chicago as a bartender. Shank and I are both working out of the Columbus, Ohio, Local Union. We're doing all right. We know you retired from the Pennsylvania National Guard Unit. We transferred to the Ohio branch. Congratulations on your new job, and I hope everything stays safe. Jon is still not satisfied with how the government is running things, as far as the military. Jon is now not only upset about the Western presence and intervention, but with the drones that are continually flying as predators that are sent to kill known Muslim officers, also killing noncombatant civilians. He says Western bombings of Muslims would obviously provoke even more anti-Western sentiment, the fuel for terrorism. One predator was intended for surveillance but was adapted for bombing specifically to kill Osama bin Laden. When bin Laden was finally found, the drone was considered too inaccurate a device to risk, and old-fashioned boots-with-guns were used. Navy Seals had to be sent to do the reassuring job."

Unmanned drones were now sweeping the global arms market. There were some ten thousand said to be in service, of which most were armed and mostly American. Unfortunately, drone war was then the flavor of the times and the military-industrial complexes were licking their lips.

"That is sad," shouted Thurston. "It's hard to imagine any greater danger to world peace than programmed armed drones flying over the Middle East. Do they still call you Blade, Joe?"

"Yeah, most people call me Blade, Thurston. Some things never change. Well, Shank and I are heading home. Hope to see you sometime, Thurston. Bye," said Joe Cipra, breaking the connection.

CHAPTER 34

The next year passed quickly, and on the end of July of 2012, Daiq had flown Thurston and Judy on the same private jet back to Florida to the Orlando Executive Airport in Central Florida. This time, they were transported to Bartow's Holiday Inn Express in a huge Cadillac SUV, also for their private use along with a driver. Vicky, Thurston's youngest daughter, was on the trip with them.

August 1 was Rie Guy's fourteenth birthday, and they were planning a huge party. Pinka and her husband were coming on a separate flight along with their two children, Samuel and Anna, which Daiq also booked. The Cadillac SUV would pick them up on their arrival. Daiq had bought Rie Guy a new expensive Fender guitar, and everyone else had got him some leisure clothing. Rie Guy had become almost like a son to Daiq. Lola loved her big brother Riley and thought that no one could compare. Jon and Cathy were just taking everything as it came in amazement. They all sat around and talked for hours while Rie Guy and Samuel messed with his new guitar and played video games. Anna and Lola were entertaining themselves by playing with Lola's huge doll collection. Daiq had a full feeling of family with Thurston's fantastic group of children and grandchildren. He loved them all.

"I did a huge write-up on Rie Guy, but I sort of gave up on *Rolling Stone* magazine. In recent years, the magazine has resumed its traditional mix of content. A UK magazine, *American Rock* accepted the story, and it will be in the next month's issue. Other celebrities have gotten a kickoff in this magazine. One famous British guitarist and pianist, I believe his name was Blackshaw, who did finger-picking techniques to create instrumental music that was both hypnotic and emotional, actually got his start there. Anyhow, we will see where the write-up goes. If you tracked down this Blackshaw, he could possibly be related to Rie Guy because of his mother's ancestry."

"Is there anything that you can't do?" asked Judy. "You are like a magic genie that popped out of a bottle and is granting wishes. Even Annabelle and Charley have made comments about how you carry yourself and spread good cheer everywhere you go. It's magic, you are heaven sent."

"I have been blessed with a gift of gab and an overabundant amount of wealth, but it all comes from being in the right places at the right time. I truly enjoy spreading my wealth in hopes of stopping all the unrest in the world. I appreciate what Thurston is doing for us at the power plant, and he should be rewarded for his loyalty."

"We're all proud of Fuge, that's what the grandkids call him. He has always been good to Mimi, that's what the grandkids call Mom and to his three daughters when we were coming up," said Cathy, smiling at Daiq.

Judy said, rolling her eyes, "Yes, he's a constant laugh, sometimes aggravating with his quotes and sayings, and repeating, oh my God!"

"As I said many times before, I never repeat myself," said Thurston.

"Very funny, how long do you have to stay at the power plant, Dad? That place always scared the life out of me," asked Pinka, doing a slight shiver with her shoulders.

"They told me a minimum of two years," answered Thurston. "Then I am retiring for good."

"Hey, guess what, Rie Guy and his garage band have a gig at a place called the Venue in Lakeland, Florida," exclaimed Cathy as she showed everyone a brochure of the Venue. "Their band sent in a demo, and they want to take a look at them."

"That is great," responded Daiq. "I love venues where they take a look at all the local talent. I always remember The Half Moon Putney in Putney, London. It was a well-known venue that offered lunchtime and evening performances. Venues are just fantastic."

"That will be a good opportunity for them to show off," yelled Vicky, clapping her hands and doing some dance moves.

"Cathy and I wouldn't miss this for the world. This is Rie Guy's debut and just the beginning. I see many gigs after this one," bragged Jon, strutting around like a proud father.

"All right," shouted Michael Trainer, twirling his hand above his head. "We got ourselves a fourteen-year-old rock star now, don't we?"

CHAPTER 35

Thurston had done the chief executive of operations job for over a year and a half. He was happy that his tenure at the power plant was about over. He was certainly worried because he had a sneaky suspicion that the troubles at the plant weren't over. Everything seemed to be peaceful at this point.

"Another six months, and you'll be out of there, Thurston," said Judy as she rolled over onto her elbow and looked up at him. "You always said it was good to be the king."

"Well, heavy is the head that wears the crown," replied Thurston. "I've had this reoccurring dream that is spooky. The dream begins after hearing reports of a radical revolutionary group threatening to strike soon, and I became convinced that they were going to target a nuclear power plant. I am at the plant and militants kill the facilities private-security guards and made their way to the Bunker where two modules are stored. They hooked up and removed the modules, which would probably be air-lifted, then made their way to the plant's reactor. Federal law-enforcement personnel rush to the scene, but it's too late. The terrorists trigger a full-scale nuclear meltdown, killing tens of thousands of people and rendering cities uninhabitable for decades."

"What a terrible dream, you don't think something like that is going to happen at your plant, do you?" asked Judy, wishing that Thurston wouldn't have taken that job.

"Nuclear-related terrorism fears are nothing new. Before the September 11 attacks, Al-Qaeda ringleader Mohamed Atta considered trying to crash a hijacked airliner into a nuclear power plant near New York City. Atta dropped the idea, but military and law-enforcement personnel believe that Al-Qaeda and other groups continue to dream of one day mounting a successful strike on a US nuclear plant. I sure hope they hold off for a few years. I don't want to achieve immortality through my work. I want to achieve immortality through not dying. I believe Woody Allen once said that, didn't he?"

"You are scaring the crap out of me," yelled Judy, shaking her head and wanting to ease that talk up a little. "Stop it with your sayings, Woody Allen, indeed. I thought you were dropped on your head as a baby, but you were clearly flung against the wall. You can't tell me all those things and expect me to feel good about you working at the power plant."

"Don't worry, if anything was going to happen, it would have happened by now," replied Thurston, waving Judy off and smiling. "You have to agree that things have been relatively calm."

"If I agreed with you…we would both end up being wrong? I still believe there was more going on with Albert Fu Fu then has come to light. I suggest you keep that security group alert until you can get out of there."

CHAPTER 36

September 11, 2012, the American diplomatic mission at Benghazi, in Libya, was attacked by a heavily armed group. The attack began during the night at a compound that is meant to protect the consulate building. Four people were killed, including the United States ambassador. Ten others were injured. The attack was strongly condemned by the governments of Libya, the United States, and many other countries throughout the world.

Originally, an embassy referred to an ambassador and his staff who were sent by their country to another countries government to represent and advance the interests of their own country. Today, the embassy is the nerve center of affairs inside another country. An embassy is usually located in the capital city of a foreign nation. United States embassies abroad, as well as foreign embassies in the United States, have a special status. While an embassy remains the territory of the host country, under international rules, representatives of the host country may not enter the embassy without permission. Because an embassy represents a sovereign state, any attack on an embassy is considered an attack on the country it represents.

The Benghazi attack consisted of military assaults on two separate US diplomatic compounds. The first assault occurred at the main compound, at approximately 9:40 pm. The second assault took place at a CIA annex, 1.2 miles away at about 4:00 am the following morning. A diplomatic security service special agent, Scott Strickland, had secured Ambassador J. Christopher Stevens and an information management officer, Sean Smith, in the main compound's safe haven. Militant attackers entered the main compound and crashed the locked metal grille of the safe haven. They were carrying jerry cans of diesel fuel, spread the fuel over the floor and furniture, and set fires. Apparently, Strickland, Stevens, and Smith decided to leave the safe haven after being overcome with smoke. Strickland exited through a window, but Ambassador Stevens and Smith did not follow him. Three other agents from the diplomatic security service returned to the main compound in an armored vehicle; they searched the building and found Sean Smith, who was unconscious and later declared dead from asphyxiation caused by smoke inhalation. Some Libyans later found the ambassador's body in a smoke-filled room and rushed him to the Benghazi Medical Center. He was also pronounced dead by Dr. Ziad Abu Zeid at the medical center from severe asphyxiation.

"When I first heard about it, Thurston," replied Daiq, "I honestly thought that all four that were killed in the Benghazi attack were blown up in a car, here Ambassador Stevens and Sean Smith died in the main compound of asphyxiation, go figure. In addition, two of the four men who died in the September 11 attack, former Navy Seal commandos Tyrone Woods and Glen Doherty, were actually CIA contractors. They arrived from Tripoli with a CIA-led reinforcement team at 4:00 am and immediately took up defensive positions at the CIA annex. Woods and Doherty defended the base from a roof and were killed when the militants launched a brief but deadly mortar attack. Unreal, how do you see it, Thurston?"

"The way I see it, Daiq," said Thurston as he switched the phone to his right ear. "When our embassy grounds are being attacked and being breached, the first response of the United States must be outrage at the breach of the sovereignty of our nation. You cannot let something like this stand. Those militants need to be brought to justice swiftly. We need to send a very clear message that we will not tolerate this kind of activity and taking the life of a US diplomat anywhere in the world. This needs to happen quickly."

"Well, Thurston," exclaimed Daiq. "Your president said, 'Make no mistake. We will work with the Libyan government to bring justice to killers that attack our people.' Do you believe that? Is that acting quickly?"

"Yeah, right," said Thurston, looking disgusted. "Talk to you later."

"Bye."

"United States Intelligence agencies say they have found no evidence of Al-Qaeda participation, but I still feel that Al-Qaeda ordered the attack," replied Jon when

Thurston called him later. "We keep looking weaker as a nation. That is a fact."

"It was quite a coincidence that the attack occurred on the eleventh anniversary of the September 11 attack in New York City," recalled Thurston. "I have to agree that there was some involvement of Al-Qaeda, even if they were not there in body."

"For sure, anyway, the kids are doing great and tell Daiq that we thank him for everything that he has done for us. Okay, Thurston, we'll be talking to you later. Bye."

CHAPTER 37

It was now May of 2013. Thurston was still in charge of the power plant. Thurston and Annabelle were enjoying morning coffee and having a hot discussion about gun control with Richard Vixen and Charley Scott. They were in Jill Walinski's office, which was adjacent to the security office where they could see all of the monitor screens for all areas of the plant.

"I'm afraid these gun-control efforts, while noble, would only have a modest impact on the rate of gun violence in America," stated Annabelle. "If the United States were as mature as the countries of Europe, where strict gun control is the norm, the federal government would have a much easier time curtailing the average citizen's access to weapons."

"That's crap, Annabelle," argued Richard, waving her off. "How do we reduce gun crime and Aurora-style mass shootings when Americans own nearly 300 million firearms? Maybe by allowing more people to carry weapons! Anti-gun activists believe the expansion of concealed-carry permits represents a serious threat to public order. But what if, in fact, the reverse is true? Mightn't letting more law-abiding private citizens to carry concealed weapons…when combined with other forms of stringent gun regulation…actually reduce gun violence?" What do you think, Thurston?"

"Thomas Jefferson once said, 'Occasionally the tree of Liberty must be watered with the blood of Patriots and Tyrants.' Certainly one of the chief guarantees of freedom is the right for citizens to keep and bear arms…. The right to bear arms is just one guarantee to protect ourselves against the rule of a tyrant or absolute ruler," answered Thurston as he walked over to the coffee pot to refill his cup. "We have a right to protect ourselves against militants and misdirected people, but assault weapons with drum-style magazines, which can hold up to one hundred rounds of ammunition and make continuous firing easy, have no reasonable civilian purpose. None! Their sale could be eliminated without violating the Second Amendment rights of individual gun owners. That is what I would call gun control, or at least a start."

Richard burst out, "Clint Eastwood had the best quote, he said, 'I have a strict gun control policy: If there's a gun around, I want to be in complete control of it.'"

"That's my sentiments exactly," Annabelle laughed. "I'd rather have my gun ready and not need it than to need it and not have it. What about you, Charley?"

Charley tried to sound enthusiastic. "I live in London, and I love living in a gun-free environment and long may it continue. But I am trained and have a concealed-carry permit because I am a security officer, and I would not hesitate to use my gun to protect myself or others from harm."

"I honestly believe in the National Rifle Association," said Thurston. "The National Rifle Association is one of the United States' largest certifying bodies for firearm safety training and proficiency training for police departments, recreational hunting, and child firearm safety. The National Rifle Association publishes several magazines and sponsors marksmanship events featuring shooting skills."

The National Rifle Association of America (NRA) is an American nonprofit organization founded in 1871 that promotes the right of citizens to bear arms, as well as police training, firearm safety, marksmanship, hunting, and self-defense training in the United States. The NRA's political activity is based on the idea that firearm ownership is a civil right protected by the Second Amendment of the bill of rights. The group has nearly century-long record of influencing as well as lobbying for or against proposed firearm legislation on behalf of its members. The National Rifle Association has reached over four million members.

In 2012, following the Sandy Hook Elementary School shooting, the National Rifle Association called on the United States Congress to appropriate funds for a "National School Shield Program," under which armed police officers would protect students in every US school. The National Rifle Association announced the creation of a program for best practices in all areas of security, building design, access control, information technology, and student and teacher training.

"Well, enough about gun control, I need to find Hoy Lee Chong and John Howard," said Richard, throwing his Styrofoam cup in the wastebasket. "Those two are inseparable, and they are constantly talking about the use of nuclear energy in thirty-one countries and naval vessels using nuclear propulsion. The proponents and environmentalists contend that nuclear power is a sustainable energy source that reduces carbon emissions and the opponents, such as Greenspan International who believe that nuclear power poses many threats to people and the environment. I've been around those guys so much lately that I'm starting to sound like them. Anyway, I'll talk to you later."

Richard was making his way over to the no. 2 reactor when he heard a huge explosion that almost knocked him off his feet. The echoing warning beepers were going off so loud that he could barely think. He instinctively ran toward the exit to get out of the building, thinking that one of the reactors may be exploding. When he busted out the exit door, all he could see in the direction of the front gate was a huge cloud of black smoke. He could see that the guard building was completely gone and huge army vehicles with enormous rubber tires were coming through the smoke. Two tanks followed and were going in the direction of the no. 2 warehouse and the Bunker. Men were jumping from the vehicles with what looked like assault weapons. They were spaying and shooting at anyone that moved. Richard pulled his weapon, but before he could get off a round, he was riddled by a flare of bullets that put him down. The tanks crashed the two sets of gates, and their machine guns cut down the three armed guards who were protecting the Bunker.

Inside the building, Hoy Lee Chong and John Howard were making their way past the operations power station to get out of the building when they spotted one of the employees messing with the controls that operated the doors of the bunker. Hoy Lee Chong pulled his weapon and yelled at that perpetrator who swung around with his own weapon and fired three shots at them, hitting John in the right knee. Hoy Lee Chong responded and dropped the man with two shots. It was too late because the doors to the Bunker were wide open, and the tanks had fired four rounds of projectiles, which penetrated the modules inside, blowing off the roof and created an enormous explosion, which caused a radioactive mushroom cloud.

"We are under attack, these people have to be on a suicide mission," yelled Chong, running to help John who could hardly walk. Everyone was panicking and trying to get out of the building and being mowed down as soon as they stepped outside. Chong helped get John to one of the exits in the rear of the building, close to the Bunker. "You stay here, John, I want to try to get some bigger weapons." Chong was shocked to see that the dead militants were Orientals and not Muslims as he would have expected. He ran out to where the dead security guards were and picked up two of their assault weapons and three extra magazines of ammunition, returning to where he had left John.

John was laying facedown apparently being shot by the terrorists. Hoy Lee Chong returned fire as he started back toward the offices where Thurston and Annabelle were. He knew that was the only way out. His radio was useless because of the noise of the warning beepers and the gunfire. Bodies were laying everywhere as he made his way through the building, shooting at the attackers wearing protective suits. Two more explosions were detonated coming from the direction of the reactors. More "dirty bombs." ("Dirty bombs" were a conventional explosive laced with radioactive material.) Clicking on his two-way radio and calling the office, Chong exclaimed, "Thurston, this is Chong. Those explosions are spewing freaking radioactive materials all over the place. We are all going to die." Chong made his way through corridors and up flights of stairs to get to the office. He had not seen Richard Vixen or Ron Reason, presuming they were dead. "Don't leave without me," yelled Chong.

CHAPTER 38

"For Christ's sake, what the hell is going on?" shouted Thurston, jumping up from his desk and running into the security office. "We're under freaking attack. We have to get some freaking help here."

"I've already put out the alert to all local authorities, the International Atomic Energy Authority, and the National Guard," shouted Charley.

"From what I'm seeing, those are all National Guard vehicles that are out there, those militants must have confiscated them from the National Guard unit by force," screamed Annabelle as she opened a cabinet full of heavy artillery firearms and magazines of ammunition. She filled her vest full of ammunition, secured an assault weapon, and handed one of the assault weapons to Charley, who slung it over his shoulder and grabbed ammunition for himself. Thurston also picked up a pistol and five clips of ammunition.

The offices were totally secure, and the overlook windows were made of special polymer materials that huge projectiles couldn't penetrate them. Annabelle said she picked up Hoy Lee Chong very faintly on the radio and couldn't understand what he was saying, but he was still alive. She scurried over to the window and couldn't believe her eyes. There was nothing but smoke and destruction. All the monitors in the security office showed the same. The entire power plant was being trashed.

"We have to get the hell out of here, Thurston," Annabelle suggested as she spotted Ron Reason sprawled out on one of the walkways, looking dead.

"Not yet, we have to wait and give Hoy Lee Chong and John Howard a chance to get here."

"Holy freaking Christ," spurted Charley. "You aren't going to believe this. The International Atomic Energy Authority is saying that we are not the only freaking power plant being attacked."

"What the hell does that mean? You got to be shitting me, we are in the midst of major catastrophe, and all our nuclear fuel rods have to be melting down because of the explosions. We are spewing radioactive junk for miles, and you are telling me that we're not alone. What the hell."

"Thurston, I just talked to Daiq, and he is at your house with Judy," said Charley. "They are going into your concrete radiation shelter until you can pick them up. Word is out, and people are panicking all over the city."

"Okay, let's get the hell out of here."

"Wait, I see Chong coming," yelled Annabelle, motioning for Charley to get the door and let him in. "What the hell! Ron Reason just got up all bloody and is chasing after him. He must be all right."

Ron Reason caught up to Chong from behind and tackled him to the concrete walkway, trying to strangle him or bite him. His lower lip was ripped off, and his teeth were showing and he was growling.

"Get the hell off me, you freaking big goon, what are you trying to do?" shouted Chong as Ron was still trying to bite him. Chong reached around and grabbed his pistol and raised it and shot Ron Reason in the head. He pushed him away, got to his feet, and ran for the door that Charley held opened. "That man was the scariest thing I have ever seen. What the hell was wrong with him?"

"I don't know, but I think we have more company," said Jill as she was looking at the outside of the door, and there were more scary-looking creatures.

"All right, Annabelle, lead the way. Let's go," ordered Thurston as Chong grabbed a fresh assault weapon from the cabinet and five magazines of ammunition. He told Thurston that John Howard didn't make it. Annabelle raced to the wall and opened the hidden door, and the group all rushed through and down the stairs. Annabelle secured the door from her side tight enough that no one could open it. She also descended the stairs and joined the others. There were only five of them, so they fit in the transfer car comfortably, all wearing the protective clothing with self-contained breathing apparatus if needed. Annabelle drove the transfer car.

"What the hell were we seeing back there, anyway?" asked Jill. "Have you guys ever heard of zombies? That's what they looked like to me."

"That's ridiculous, no such thing," stated Charley. "Ron Reason just went into shell shock. He had no idea what he was doing. He would have killed Chong if Chong wouldn't have acted quickly. That happens to soldiers on the battlefield. They just go south."

"Speaking about going south, that is where we are going as quickly as possible. We'll stop and pick up Judy and Daiq and head toward Pittsburgh. Jill, you said you talked to your husband, and he will meet us in Robinson Township at the exit into Chestnut Ridge, we will keep in contact."

The transfer car made it the four miles where the armored vehicle waited.

"That vehicle is the size of a bus, and it doesn't look like an army vehicle," replied Chong, getting out of the car and looking closer.

"Don't be fooled by the look. This vehicle is stronger and more maneuverable than a Hummer, completely bullet- and projectile-proof and completely self-contained. It is wedged in front to remove any obstacles," Annabelle claimed. "I will not be driving that vehicle."

"I've driven vehicles like this before," said Hoy Lee Chong. "It shouldn't be that much of a task. Okay, everybody aboard."

The wedged front of the huge bus-type vehicle pushed open the hidden doors, and they found themselves on a long stretch of Route 90. Visibility wasn't great because of the smoke and dust in the air. Seemed like real heavy smog. The road was vacant for about five miles, but all at once, it became havoc. Cars were stopped and some seemed to be empty.

"We have to get off the next exit to get to my house in Stockton. Can we pass all these cars?" asked Thurston, stretching his neck to see what was going on with the traffic tie up.

"Something is real weird here, Thurston," cautioned Chong. "Looks like dead people in and around these cars."

"This is getting serious, we can't leave the bus because we can't be exposed to the radiation, and all we can do is drift through and see how far we can get. Let's go on the outside of the cars, Chong, on the same side as the exit."

As they eased past the cars, they could see the total devastation in every inch that they traveled. Men, women, children, and animals looked like mannequins lying in different positions all along the highway as far as you could see.

"Those terrorists were Oriental, Thurston, what do you make of that? I'll bet that was part of that Albert Fu Fu's scheme. I believe his negotiations were with some Oriental organization that is trying to destroy the United States. What they've done at this power plant is going to be much bigger than the Three-Mile Island incident, the Chernobyl disaster in 1986, or Japan's Fukushima nuclear power plant meltdown. Those were huge nuclear accidents, but this has the potential of being the most catastrophic ever because of the explosions and their "dirty bombs." These radioactive materials that are spewing for miles are so thick that it is knocking people dead instantly. We have to get out of this Stockton area as quickly as possible."

"We have to get through all these vehicles to pick up Judy and Daiq and definitely head south. There goes my cell phone. Hello."

"Holy shit, Thurston, where are you?" exclaimed Jon. "It's all over the news. They're saying that the Stockton power plant got completely destroyed. Are you safe? What about Judy? Is she all right?"

"We're on our way to pick her and Daiq up at our house. They're in the shelter. Things are really bad. There are dead people everywhere. There is some nasty radiation spewing out of the plant. We are in a self-contained bus trying to get the hell out of Stockton."

"Things are worse than that, those terrorists hit five other nuclear power plants besides Stockton. They blew up the Indian Point plant in Buchanan, New York, which is a major source of power for New York City, the Byron Nuclear Plant in Ogle County, Illinois, is being terrorized, which supplies power for Chicago, the Calvert Cliffs plant in Maryland, which supplies power to Washington, DC, the McGuire plant in Charlotte, and another one in Georgia. I can't freaking believe this is happening. That means the whole East Coast is getting dumped on with radiation. They have shut down some major cities. I knew if we kept messing with that Middle East that they would retaliate. I think all of us need to head west. The United States is planning on firing nuclear missiles at the president's command."

"Hoy Lee Chong says that the terrorists are Oriental. I think we're being hit by someone other than the Al-Qaeda. It's got to be China, Japan, or Korea. Anyhow we're heading south to pick up Victoria, Pinka, Mike, and the kids, and my secretary Jill's husband, then we are heading west."

CHAPTER 39

When they came to the exit, it was also backed up with cars and a tractor trailer was jackknifed on the turn. It was lying on its side and blocking the way for them to get around the cars.

"You'll have to move it with the bus, Chong, there is no other way," said Thurston, pointing to move it off to the right hand side. The bus wedged between the cab of the truck and vehicles that lined the exit and started pushing. A man suddenly jumped from behind the cab and was on the hood of the bus, scratching at the window and acting crazy. His face was bloody, and the skin was ripped from his jaw.

"What the hell," yelled Chong, steering the bus, trying to move the truck off to the side.

"Keep pushing, that must be the driver of the truck. We can't stop, and he will eventually fall off," shouted Thurston as the man was growling and trying to break the window. "We're past the truck, slam on the brake, Chong."

Chong slammed on the break, and the man flew off the front of the bus then pushed the gas down, and they were on their way.

"What are those freaking things?" screamed Chong.

"I'm telling you those are zombies. Those people are rising from the dead. Zombies are reanimated humans usually by a virus, but these are being reanimated by that radioactive junk that is killing them. These creatures are probable radioactive. Radioactive zombies," yelled Jill.

"Stop that shit, Jill," shouted Annabelle. "That is a bunch of bullshit that you're putting out there and scaring everyone shitless. Stop it!"

"Look up front, guys, before you say anything else," gasped Chong.

Up ahead, there were people walking in a peculiar manner. Along the bypass road, it looked like hundreds just roaming around.

"Christ, Jill, what else do you know about these damn things?" muttered Annabelle, starting to panic a lot.

"They are devoid of intelligence and are motivated only by the desire to consume human flesh. The only way to destroy them is to destroy their brain by any means. They are slow-moving, and they moan. According to the video games, they can be destroyed by fire, but this is no video game that we are playing. This is real. I'm scared."

"We have to go to the left up here and about a mile to my house. Just keep driving, and if they get in the way, run them over. We can't waste any more time, and if there is a God, he'll let us get there in time," Thurston yelled, finding that he was just as frightened as everyone else as the bus was closing in on his house. There were people walking in and out of the house. Thurston had on a protective suit with breathing apparatuses and grabbed two more protective suits and pulled his pistol, ready to exit the bus and go to the underground shelter in the basement of the house.

"You have to shoot them in the head, anything else is ineffective," said Jill, warning Thurston.

"Let me go with you, Thurston," pleaded Charley. "You don't know how many are in the house."

"No, you have to help get out of here. Remember, go west, the East Coast is polluted with radiation," said Thurston as the door was released, and he shot two of the creatures in the head, dropping them to the ground. He hurried to the front door and entered the house. They heard two more shots go off and then it was silent. They waited for what seemed like forever. The zombies were scratching the outside of the bus and trying to find a way in. Two more shots went off inside the house, but no one was coming out.

Finally, after two or three minutes, three protective suits emerged out of the front door and moving toward the bus door. Thurston blew four more of them away, shooting them in their heads. They boarded the bus in the decontamination section where they stripped the suits off and put them in a chamber. When the clear sign came up and the door slid open, Charley said, "Lets get the hell out of here, Chong."

"You people are a sight for sore eyes. I thought we were dead for sure. Are you the only ones that made it out of the plant?" asked Daiq, completely out of breath.

"John Howard, Richard, and Ron didn't make it," Charley said as he looked at Judy hugging Thurston real tight. "Where did you learn to shoot like that, Thurston? Quite an exhibition you put on."

"I qualified with all kinds of weapons in my thirty-year army and National Guard career. I have never actually shot anyone before."

"These don't count. They are already dead."

"The terrorists blew up five other plants besides ours, Daiq. Parts of New York, Chicago, and Washington, DC, are all without power, and who knows if they are being invaded with zombies. That is what Jill calls them. We have to head west after we do a couple of pickups. Where do you suggest we go?" asked Thurston.

"This has approached sooner than I had thought. Memphis, Tennessee, we have to get to Memphis. We need to get to Interstate 79 and stay on it. We'll make that stop in Robinson Township to pick up Victoria and Jill's husband. We continue on Interstate 79 to Morgantown and pick up Pinka and her family and follow 79 to Charleston where we pick up Route 64 west. We bypass Lexington, Kentucky, continue to Elizabethtown, and take Interstate 75 south to Nashville, and then Route 40 west to Memphis, Tennessee. Thurston, you call Jon and tell him to make it up to Memphis International Airport but tell him to go across on Route 10 west though Florida to avoid Interstate 75 through Georgia then up Interstate 55 north through Mississippi to Memphis. I need to hook up with the president."

Thurston called Jon and told him to take his family and get to the Memphis International Airport as quickly as possible. He gave him the directions to avoid Georgia, told him to pack some clothes, and said he would call later. He called Victoria and told her that Jill's husband, Stanley Walinski, would pick her up, and they would meet them at the exit going into Chestnut Ridge apartments. He told her to pack clothes and bring Winston.

"Better hurry, Dad, word is getting around fast. I believe that the great panic is going to start soon. It's all over the television."

"We're moving as fast as we can. We'll see you there."

He also called Pinka and told her pack some clothes, and they would pick her family up at the Westover exit. She would leave her vehicle there at the mall so they could get back onto the highway quickly.

Daiq was on the phone for the longest time, talking to whom Thurston thought was the president of the United States. When he returned, he told Thurston that the president had great concerns about Israel doing some kind of nuclear retaliation on the Muslim cities, thinking it is the Muslims that attacked the United States. The United States had said they are willing to go to nuclear war to protect Israel, but not having Israel bring on war by "military alliances" with their aggressive actions by using the "Samson Option." The president had said that the Pentagon is ready to launch missiles and that they are in complete control of our Missile Defense System. The United States has 2,500 warheads on alert that can be launched immediately on any warning with a range of 8,100 miles. Israel is especially dangerous because its leaders and supporters have made clear for years that if Israel or its alliances were ever devastated by any kind of war or attack, it would retaliate in indiscriminate "Samson Option" attacks on not just the Muslim cities, but against

European and even Russian targets as well. Russia, of course, would retaliate with thousands of nuclear bombs against the United States. Once there is use of nuclear weapons, it will be like giving permission for everyone to use them. Any use of nuclear weapons will probably lead to a rapid escalation, *World Nuclear War*.

"That is why we have to move quickly. Once the panic starts, we will be immobile," replied Daiq. "I have no idea what is developing with those walking dead people. My intention right now is to get all of us and Zeppy Riley somewhere safe. The coalition has thirteen different safe areas in case of nuclear attack. One is on Santa Catalina Island which is a rocky island off the coast of California. The island is located about twenty-two miles south-southwest of Los Angeles, California. Catalina is one of the Channel Islands of California archipelagos, which lies within Los Angeles County. A fortress was built many years ago on the west side of the island between the two populated centers, the island's only incorporated city, Avalon, and the unincorporated village of Two Harbors. It was purchased by the coalition and made into a self-contained development cut out of Mt. Orizaba, which is the highest point on the island at 2,097 feet, which generates its own electricity from the sun and has two helicopter landing ports with hangars, mostly underground surrounded with solid rock. It has a filtering system for water directly from the ocean, storing one hundred and fifty thousand gallons of purified water at all times. We can't use the Pittsburgh International Airport because of congestion, so our challenge is collect everyone and get to the Memphis International Airport in Memphis, Tennessee. I have arranged for a private jet to fly all of us to Denver International Airport in Denver, Colorado."

"How do you do all that so fast, Daiq? Are we at war?" asked Judy.

"I have been prepared for things like this my entire career. I have connections all over this world. The forever-asked question 'Is world nuclear war inevitable?' has been in predictions and in prophecies forever, Judy. It is of extreme importance that we protect Zeppy Riley."

"Can Jon, Cathy, and the kids fly to Memphis?" Judy asked Daiq.

"I'm glad you said that, Judy. I have a friend at the Orlando Executive Airport, Albert Bestal, who has a small private propeller plane. Let me see if I can connect with him," said Daiq as he wandered to the back of the bus to make a call. When he returned, he told Thurston to get a hold of Jon and tell him to forget about driving and make his way to the Orlando Executive Airport. The guards would be waiting for them in the morning, 7:00 am, the guards would hook them up with Albert Bestal, and he would secure their car and fly them to Memphis International Airport. "They could wait for us there. Tell Jon to keep his phone charged, that is our only contact."

"Holy shit," screamed Chong. "Look what's coming up!"

CHAPTER 40

Cathy was talking on the phone to Pinka saying how Jon had predicted that all this was going to happen if the United States kept messing with that Middle East.

"Jon seems to think that the East Coast is going to be devastated for quite a while and that Daiq said that we have to vacate for a while because he has to keep us all safe."

"All they are saying on television is not to panic, stay at home, and wait for any indicated evacuations. Dad said that we are going west until this blows over. I guess we can't worry about the kids missing school. I've packed most of their clothes. Samuel packed his Xbox and his games, naturally. He doesn't go anywhere without them. Anna wants to take the dog, Nui. We're leaving the bunny at a farm near us."

"Same thing here, Rye Guy has his guitar, amplifier, and his Xbox. I talked to Mom, and she says that they are traveling in a huge indestructible bus. She said they are traveling on Interstate 79 right now, almost to Pittsburgh. They'll be picking you up, and we are all supposed to meet at the Memphis International Airport in Memphis, Tennessee. We are being flown there by one of Daiq's friends from the Orlando Executive Airport, no less. Do you believe all this?" exclaimed Cathy. "You have to let Anna take Nui. *Nui* means *big* in Hawaiian. Our cats will exist, they run wild anyway. Rye Guy may take Remy, I don't know."

" I know that Vicky will bring Winston. Problem is, Nui eats like crazy. Oh well, I'm hoping we aren't gone that long," replied Pinka, packing a final suitcase, hoping that whatever is happening in the United States will end soon.

"Not to worry. Daiq, for some reason, has a heavy watch on Rye Guy and is determined to get him to safety. Look at the television now, Pinka, they're saying that the radiation cloud is moving toward Pittsburgh. Dad's vehicle is still on the highway moving down Interstate 79. I hope that they are listening somehow to what is happening." Jon came into the room and told Cathy that parts of New York City is being engulfed in smoke and radiation, and possibly Washington, DC.

"Thurston said that they wouldn't make it to Memphis until tomorrow morning," Jon explained. "We have to be at the airport to meet Albert Bestal at seven in the morning."

"Pinka, I'm getting off the phone now. I'm going to call Vicky to see what she knows. She is probably having a fit. See ya," exclaimed Cathy as she hurried up and punched Vicky's number.

"Bye, keep me updated."

"Vicky, this is Cathy, have you heard from Dad? Where are they?"

"Don't know, Stanley Walinski and I are watching on television, and they're saying the radiation is getting close. They should have been here, no one has called. They may be stuck in traffic. I don't want to tie up the phone. I will let you know if they make it. Bye."

CHAPTER 41

"For the love of God, we are in freaking trouble, there are thirty or forty cars piled up on that bridge by Emsworth, what the hell we do now, Thurston?" yelled Chong, putting on the brakes hard and sliding a little to the right, barely getting stopped.

"Damn it," shouted Thurston. "We have to keep going, take this next exit to Route 65. It will take us to Sewickley, Pennsylvania. I know how to get to the Chestnut Ridge Apartment from there."

Chong swung the bus to the inside edge of the road and made his way to the exit, bumping a couple of cars on the way. A policeman was signaling for them to stop, but Thurston told Chong to keep going. They made it onto the exit and followed Route 65 to Sewickley, crossed the Ohio River, and continued through Moon Township to Robinson Township. Thurston called Vicky and told her to meet them in ten minutes as they took the back way through Settlers Park to get there. Vicky and Stanley boarded the bus quickly. Vicky was carrying her suitcase and Winston. They traversed down to the entry ramp to the parkway toward Pittsburgh and pushed and banged there way to the exit for Interstate 79 again. As they were building up speed, it began to get dark. It was 5:30 pm, and everyone was getting hungry.

"We can stop in Washington, Pennsylvania, and get some fast food. The only food on the bus is in cans and cartons. We are not that desperate yet," replied Judy, holding her nose.

"Yes," said Annabelle, agreeing with Judy. "I hope we can all relax for a while, this has been a rough ride."

Thurston said, "We still have a long way to go, there may be more trouble. Make the stop in Washington quick. We still have another pick up in Morgantown."

They grabbed there fast sandwiches and drinks, went across the Route 70 bypass and got on Interstate 79 once again. Chong had the bus going seventy-five miles per hour and passed quite a few cars. Thurston called Pinka and told her to get to the Westover exit; they would be there soon. They would leave their vehicle at the mall. The pick up went like clockwork, and they were on their way to Charleston, West Virginia. The reports on the radio weren't sounding good. The Pittsburgh International Airport was shut down to flights because of the overabundance of angry people breaching the checkpoint, trying to get aboard. They had to call in extra security. The highways all around Pittsburgh were now completely tied up. The people are now being told to evacuate. Go figure.

"We escaped that mess in Pittsburgh pretty smooth, also good that we didn't go toward the airport. We still have about fifteen to sixteen hours of travel, so we'll have to trade off driving until we get to Memphis International Airport. Chong, why don't you get some rest, and I will drive for a while," suggested Daiq. "We'll try to pick up some extra clothing for everyone when we get to the San Bernardino International Airport. It is located less then two miles southwest of the city center of San Bernardino, California. We should have some time there."

The time was dragging as they made it to Charleston. They took the bypass around Charleston and picked up Route 64 going west to Lexington, Kentucky, around the bypass at Lexington and picked up the Blue Grass Parkway west to Elizabethtown, Kentucky. From Elizabethtown, they went south on Route 65 to Nashville, Tennessee, around the bypass and picked up Route 40 west to Memphis. Thurston relieved Daiq, Charley relieved Thurston, Annabelle relieved Charley, and Daiq took over again when they were approaching Memphis, Tennessee. They went around the bypass to Route 55 south, close to the Memphis International Airport. It was 9:15 am, and Thurston called Jon. They were waiting at the arrivals where the bus stopped and picked them up and headed toward the private flights area. Daiq made some contacts, and all their luggage was picked up and loaded. A large carrying cage was brought for Nui. Vicky could carry Winston. Daiq drove the bus to the loading zone, but Annabelle said there was more trouble. She couldn't get Chong up, and he was acting delirious and talking strange. Charley and Annabelle helped Chong and they all loaded onto the private jet. The yard people secured the bus, and the plane began taxiing for the runway for their flight to Denver International Airport in Denver, Colorado. They all ate breakfast on the flight, courtesy of the airline.

Thurston said that Chong might be having a late reaction to the radioactive junk he was breathing at the plant. Daiq asked Rie Guy to come into the back of the plane where Chong was lying flat on his back.

"I believe that he is going to expire, Rie," Daiq said, being very mellow. "What I need is for you to place your hand on his head and say these words, 'Arise, Chong, you are clean.'"

Rie Guy did as Daiq requested. A few minutes passed, Chong's eyes came open, and he sat up.

"What's going on? Why am I on the floor? Where are we? Rye Guy, Daiq, we made it to the plane apparently. I must have passed out."

"You must have been really tired. You've been sleeping all this time. We helped you onto the plane. We are on our way to Denver, Colorado," replied Daiq, helping him get to his feet. "How do you feel now? Are you hungry?"

"Yes, I am, thanks for helping me onto the plane."

Everyone was surprised and happy to see that Hoy Lee Chong Grant had recovered. When they arrived in Denver, they were transferred to another flight heading for San Bernardino International Airport. San Bernardino International Airport is a public airport located less than two miles southeast of the city center of San Bernardino, California. At San Bernardino International Airport, Daiq had arranged for a bus-size vehicle to pick them up with their luggage and their two dogs in carrying cases. The bus would be at their disposal. They were being transported to the Hilton Garden Inn Hotel right in the center of the business District. Daiq had reserved eight queen rooms and one executive suite for himself, all on the top floor. Nui and Winston would have to stay in the hotel kennel because they weren't allowed to stay in the rooms.

"Winston wouldn't hurt anything. I wish I could keep him with me," complained Vicky, looking at Thurston for some help.

"Why can't Nui stay with us?" cried Anna.

"Those are the hotel rules, and we have to abide by them," explained Thurston. "You can go see them anytime at the kennel."

The trip wasn't very long from the airport to the hotel. They circled around the airport on S. Del Rose circle and made a right on E. Paul Villasener Blvd., then a left to Tippecanoe Ave., and another quick right on E. Mill St., taking them to S. Waterman Ave. They made a left turn on S. Waterman Ave., passed the San Bernardino Golf Club, and crossed a bridge over the Santa Ana River. They went about two miles in total, and they were at the Hilton Garden Inn Hotel. Everyone got settled in their rooms, and Daiq said that they would all go shopping for some clothes in the afternoon.

"Do you think this is the start of the end, I mean, all of this is really working on my nerves?" asked Judy as she looked at Thurston with tired, sad eyes. "Daiq seems like the only hope that we have. I'm scared."

"God is a comedian playing to an audience too afraid to laugh," replied Thurston, thinking of what Voltaire said in the 1700s. "I don't know why we are here in San Bernardino, but I'm pretty sure that it is not in order to enjoy ourselves. I'm only sure of one thing. The only reason that we are all here is because of Rie Guy. Daiq has a complete trust in him and knows much more than what he is saying. I'm new, but I'm not brand new. I was born at night, but not last night."

"Will you give all of that a rest, if brains were taxed… you'd get a rebate. Have you called your brothers?"

"Yes, Levi and Elaine are actually in Germany on vacation. I told him that he better stay there. He said that there flight to Pittsburgh was canceled already, and they were planning on flying to Fort Worth, Texas, and stay with his son, Jerry. I talked to Larry, and he still doesn't know what he and Mary are doing. I told him not to wait too long to get out of there."

"I called my brother K, and they have all gone to North Carolina for now, until they get the clearance to go back. I got no answer from Harold. I made a few other calls and couldn't get through."

"Better freshen up. Daiq is taking us shopping," shouted Thurston, thinking that he really needed to get out of the suit he was wearing.

"The shopping spree took about two hours. Everyone grabbed three or four outfits, shoes, boots, sweatshirts, and jackets. They all had their way with all the expensive shops, and Daiq picked up the tab. They went to a huge buffet and everyone ate to their heart's content. Daiq said a little prayer and picked up the tab, naturally. On the way back to the hotel, Daiq said he wanted to talk to Jon, Thurston, and Zeppy Riley in his private room.

CHAPTER 42

It was 6:00 pm when Jon, Thurston, and Rie Guy were knocking on Daiq's door at the executive suite.

"Who is it?" said a voice from inside, sounding like Daiq.

"Zeppy Riley," replied Thurston quietly, remembering the code.

The door opened, and Daiq greeted them all with a hug. Charley and Annabelle were seated in an area that would be the living quarters.

"I hope you don't mind Charley and Annabelle being here. They are part of the coalition. They are aware of everything that has gone down. First, we are making a temporary move onto Catalina Island at the underground fortress until we get more information. We have just heard that Israel has made a move that we were hoping wouldn't happen. They have fired ballistic missiles at five capital cities in the Middle East and North Africa, also Benghazi, Libya. They blasted Tehran, Iran; Baghdad, Iraq; Kabul, Afghanistan; Tripoli, Libya; and Cairo, Egypt. Those countries had no defense against the missiles."

An antiballistic missile is a missile to counter ballistic missiles (a missile for missile defense). There were no such missiles in the Middle East or Northern Africa. A ballistic missile is used to deliver nuclear, biological, or conventional warheads in a ballistic flight trajectory. The term "antiballistic missile" describes any antimissile system designed to counter ballistic missiles. The term is used more for systems designed to counter intercontinental ballistic missiles.

"Fear of Israel has stopped Russia and the other six nations having nuclear weapons [excluding the United States] from retaliating in any way, knowing that the United States had been attacked," Daiq continued. "North Korea, on the other hand, is firing ballistic missiles toward France, China, Israel, and Russia. They are all using there antiballistic defense systems to knock down North Korea's ballistic missiles. They are now trying to reach the United States with their intercontinental ballistic missiles, which no nation realized they had, targeting New York City and Washington, DC. The United States is countering the intercontinental ballistic missiles [ICBMs], with their antiballistic defense system from their ground-based midcourse defense system and their Aegis Ballistic Missile Defense with antiballistic missiles launched from a US navy *Ticonderoga*-class cruiser."

Charley added, "North Korea wants world power by destroying nuclear weapon–holding nations."

"Un freaking real," stated Jon. "We put our heads in a noose at the Stockton Nuclear Power Plant to bring awareness to madmen and tyrants in North Korea, Northern Africa, southeastern Europe, and the Middle East, sum-bitch."

"I am aware of that, and we have been watching North Korea for quite a while, Thurston. We have discovered something about Rie Guy that we have to discuss. I'm glad that you are here, Jon. Zeppy Riley may have to answer his calling at a younger age than we predicted. He has a God-given power of healing. He is not Christ or the fictitious anti-Christ of Nostradamus."

"No way," replied Thurston, thinking that Rie Guy was too young for any calling; he hasn't begun to live. No freaking way.

"I was going to ask you about that, Mr. Daiquiri. What happened when Hoy Lee Chong mysteriously recovered after I touched his head and repeated what you said?" asked Rie Guy, talking like a concerned adult.

"Chong was very close to dying, I mean seconds. You touched him and the two of you glowed, and he became free of the tainted radiation that he had inhaled at the power plant. You saved him from certain death. He was clean. Sometimes the calling is sooner than later."

"Bullshit," said Thurston. "That is impossible."

Jon said, "I don't know Thurston, I've seen Rie Guy revive or cure animals that I thought were dusters. There could be something to this."

"Absolutely, Jon, now we need to get everyone together again. I have called for a helicopter to pick all of us up and take us to the island. Another thing, Thurston, you, and Jon signed contracts about Zeppy Riley. Think hard about it. Everything relating to Rie Guy, that we talked about before, will still happen. The education and military training will happen when he comes of age. The money is still there, and your pension from the power plant will be government secured. Zeppy Riley's calling will not affect his high school education, but he also has a healing job to do. Not to worry. He will continue his schooling here in California, if this state stays clean. Every one of you can relocate here. Thurston, it is time you retire, and we can furnish jobs for anyone who wants to stay here in California. Homes will be furnished anywhere for all of you in San Bernardino or Los Angeles, Malibu, anywhere you choose, cost-free. Are you following this, Thurston?"

"Enough said, Daiq," answered Thurston. "Let's get this show on the road. I have full trust in you, Daiq."

"All right, the helicopter is waiting on the landing port in the back of the Hilton Garden Inn Hotel. Have everyone bring all their bags and articles that they want down to the lobby of the hotel. The luggage will be delivered to the helicopter, and the vehicle will return and get everyone aboard, including the dogs. I will be waiting."

They lifted off the ground with everyone totally frightened and flew over Los Angeles. It was beautiful. At one point, Stanley Walinski began to cry and was shaking like a leaf.

"What's wrong with you?" asked Jill as she was shaking him and trying to get him under control. "Everything is going to be all right."

"Bullshit," yelled Stanley. "We're all going to die, you freaking bitch. You got me into all this. I hate you. Get me back to that hotel right now, you motherless pricks. You people have to get me off this chopper, now.

"Whoa, settle down, Stanley," shouted Chong, holding him down. "You have to settle down. We will get you back if that's what you want, but you can't endanger the lives of people on board. Just sit their and be quiet."

"I'm sorry, everybody. Stanley has reached his limit with me and everything with our marriage. He told me he wanted a divorce. I wish he wouldn't have gotten on this ride. Please take him back. He's lost all touch with reality. Please let me stay with you, Thurston, he will definitely harm me. Stanley and I have only been married for a month. He is really angry. I had no idea what he was like. Please let him go."

Daiq signaled the pilot to make a turn and go back to the hotel. Daiq used his cell phone, and Jill gave him the number of Stanley's parents.

"Mr. Walinsky, this is Benjamin Daiquiri, I am a lawyer from London. Stanley, your son, came to California with us in order to get away from the East Coast. We have to complete our mission, but Stanley will be in the care of a nursing station at the Hilton Garden Inn Hotel in San Bernardino, California, and we think that he was having a mental breakdown."

The Walinski's apologized and said no problem. "He's a Vietnam veteran and has been sick for a while. The government got him that job in Pittsburgh, Pennsylvania, after suffering an injury from the war in Nam. Stanley told us that he was getting married, and we sent him some money. We will make our way to San Bernardino and pick him up." The parents lived in Dallas, Texas.

The helicopter circled, and they returned to the hotel in about fifteen minutes. Jon and Daiq helped Stanley to the nurses' station at the hotel. Daiq gave the attendants his name and told them that the parents would pick him up. He thanked them, and he and Jon returned to the helicopter.

"That man needs some help," said Jon as they boarded and they lifted off again. "Thank God for little favors."

"They will take good care of him, I'm sure. I absolutely would not let Jill go with him, agreed?" asked Daiq.

"Yes, agreed."

Rie Guy told Jill to come and sit next to him and Lola.

"Don't worry, Jill," said Rie Guy. "Lola and I will take care of you."

"Yeah," parroted Lola, giggling. "Me and Riley. He's my big brother."

"Thanks," said Jill, smiling. "I needed that."

At that very moment, Daiq got a call on his cell phone, and he went up to the captain's cockpit to answer. One of the intercontinental chemical warhead missiles made it through their ground-based midcourse defense system and their Aegis Ballistic Missile Defense with antiballistic missiles launched from a US navy *Ticonderoga*-class cruiser. The missile was bound for New York and was knocked off its ballistic flight trajectory and blasted a city on its course, Stockton, Pennsylvania.

CHAPTER 43

There were twenty-four regular people working for Daiq at the Fortress on Santa Catalina Island. There were pilots, a doctor, cooks, and maids; the whole place was completely furnished. The island is located about twenty-two miles south-southwest of Los Angeles, California. Catalina is one of the Channel Islands of California archipelagos, which lies within Los Angeles County.

When they reached the fortress, everyone was amazed. It was hidden on the dark side of the mountain, yet it would get the morning sun. It was secretly constructed; even the people on the island were unaware of its existence. The large living area was huge and had a large wall computer monitor with a state-of-the-art communication system—Internet communication, which was a faster speed that Rie Guy had never encountered in all the years that he had done Face book, YouTube, games, whatever. Instant Google or satellite to look at mapping and zooms to anywhere in the world. It was, indeed, technology that viewed telescopic images of landscapes in the United States and all over the world from satellites.

Rie Guy was ecstatic. He was clicking on icons and dropdown menus. He did searches on the Internet, clicking and dragging things across the screen. He was also elated about being around Jill and having someone to relate to. Jill was almost as tall as Rie Guy, gorgeous long blond hair, beautiful blue eyes, and a wide smile, exposing clean, pearly white teeth.

Rie Guy had a weakness for blonds. They talked about his music, he showed her his face book and all the videos he had on YouTube. Jill loved rock 'n roll, and she was totally impressed when Rie Guy showed her his guitar and amplifier. He played some music. They talked about the zombie action that had occurred in Stockton, Pennsylvania, at the power plant. He told her he knew everything about zombies and how to destroy them. He showed her on the Internet and on Xbox. Actual thoughts exchanged between them and fictional games. They had a crowd with them most of the time, Lola, his cousins Anna and Samuel, Pinka and Michael, Cathy and Jon, Annabelle and Charley, Judy and Thurston, Vicky, Daiq, and of course, Hoy Lee Chong Grant. Everyone was fascinated with all that Rie Guy had captured and how he could operate different facets of the computer. When the girls and all the kids found something else to do and watched cartoons on regular TV, Rie Guy looked at the damages at the Stockton Nuclear Power Plant. It was devastating to see. Just devastating!

"How in the hell did you five get out of there. Look, it is almost crushed to the ground, looks like the whole city of Stockton is wiped out," responded Jon, not believing his eyes. He had his arm around Rie Guy's shoulders, as Rie Guy flicked through different images of Stockton.

"Something is weird, Rie Guy," barked Thurston, pointing at the screen. "Go to the other nuclear power plant disasters. We can barely see Stockton because of the dust and smoke."

Jill was watching. Samuel was sitting with Charley and Chong. Rie Guy was clicking on icons and drop-down menus again and brought up the Indian Point plant in Buchanan, New York. It looks clear except for a little smoke, buildings seemed stable. Bryon Nuclear Power Plant in Ogle County, Illinois, Clear. The Calvert Cliffs Plant in Maryland, Clear. Charlotte, North Carolina, and Georgia, all of them clear.

"Something definitely happened in Stockton. All the other places show remains, and sadly, dead bodies, but everything is there," yelled Thurston.

"I believe I can explain that," interrupted Daiq as he popped out of a back bathroom. "Stockton was hit with a chemical ballistic missile that was bound for New York and was knocked off its ballistic flight trajectory by a near-miss defense missile and blasted Stockton, go figure. The military that has been keeping Stockton at bay is reporting that there are no more walking around creatures. They are all gone, completely blown away. Can you believe it? I believe God had something to do with that. How do you see it, Thurston?"

"Gads, do you think we and the United States Government are the only ones that knew about the walking dead that we witnessed?" asked Thurston.

"What walking dead?" answered Daiq. "All I remember is making our way and trying to get as far as we could from the East Coast for safety. Whatever happened in Stockton, Pennsylvania, after we vacated is a definite mystery to us. We are still on the verge of a nuclear freaking world war. We are at the mercy of how long it will continue. All we can do now is wait and watch. Right, Judy?"

"Yes, Daiq, just wait and watch," repeated Judy.

CHAPTER 44

Rie Guy switched to CNN live, and the president was talking to Israel, our nation, and the world, repeating some of what he said earlier in the year during Passover in Israel. (Remarks in Jerusalem on March 21, 2013). It was now a recorded video being played repeatedly.

> You know, we have bonds between our country and Israel with Israel's prime minister and their president. I am repeating some remarks from a speech I made when I went to Israel on the eve of a sacred holiday...the celebration of Passover.
>
> Of course, even as we draw strength from the story of God's will and his gift of freedom expressed on Passover, we also know that here on Earth, we must bear our responsibilities in an imperfect world. That means accepting our measure of sacrifice and struggle, just like previous generations. It means us working through generation after generation on behalf of that ideal of freedom.
>
> For the Jewish people, the journey to the promise of the state of Israel wound through

countless generations. It involved centuries of suffering and exile, prejudice and pogroms, and even genocide. Through it all, the Jewish people sustained their unique identity and traditions, as well as a longing to return home. And while Jews achieved extraordinary success in many parts of the world, the dream of true freedom finally found its full expression in the Zionist idea...to be a free people in their homeland.

Now, I stand here today mindful that for both our nations, these are some complicated times. We have difficult issues to work through within our own countries, and we face dangers and upheaval around the world. And since then, we've built a friendship that advances our shared interests. Together, we shared a commitment to security for our citizens and the stability of the Middle East and North Africa. Together, we share a focus on advancing economic growth around the globe and strengthening the middle class within our own countries. Together, we share a stake in the success of democracy, particularly as we emerge from two wars and the worst recession since the Great Depression.

This is the story of Israel. This is the work that has brought the dreams of so many generations to life. And every step of the way, Israel has built unbreakable bonds of friendship with our country, the United States of America.

And Israel has achieved all this even as it's overcome relentless threats to its security, through the courage of the Israel Defense Forces and a citizenry that is so resilient in the face of terror.

And since then, we've built a friendship that advances our shared interests. Together, we share a commitment to security for our citizens and the stability of the Middle East and North Africa. Together, we share a focus on advancing economic growth around the globe and strengthening the middle class within our own countries. Together, we share a stake in the success of democracy.

Now, the United States has been attacked by terrorists who we have identified as Oriental. These attacks are outrageous and shocking. The bombing in the Middle East and North Africa only came as retaliation from Israel because of 'military alliances' to the United States for the constant terrorism that we have both encountered. We are now under intercontinental ballistic missile attacks in the United States and ballistic missiles all over the world. They are coming from the direction of North Korea. Make no mistake, justice will be done. We are asking for an unconditional stop to the firing of ballistic missiles with nuclear warheads and all bombings until we can sort these things out. We don't want a 'nuclear world war.' Thank you, and God bless all of you.

The United States was still countering with their antiballistic missile systems when the stream of missiles stopped. Russia, France, England had blasted North Korea with tons of ballistic missiles with nuclear warheads from their launching stations. North Korea could not counter the amount of missiles that were coming toward them.

They were being trashed. Russian and United States "predator drones" zoomed in and spotted the launching pad targets. The president of the United States could be proud of what he had accomplished in his speech. North Korea was unconditionally defeated. The missile world had become silent. The president of the United States had quoted in his speech, "Make no mistake, justice will be done."

CHAPTER 45

"Thurston, Jon, you aren't going to believe this. All the countries are in agreement to give Israel immunity for the nuclear ballistic missiles that they dumped on the Middle East and North Africa," shouted Daiq, running and trying to get everyone together. "Israel has apologized for the retaliation, but they had warned those countries that it would happen. Sometimes we react to the places that continually threaten us. Strong military alliances will go nuclear to protect each other. This has been quite a scare showing what could have gone to 'world nuclear war' that could last for years and bring everything to a definite end. All the countries that definitely have nuclear weapons are continuing de facto nuclear proliferation and are agreeing to make progress on serious nuclear disarmament. Maybe this is the awakening that was needed. It will take years to clear and rejuvenate these countries and to bury their dead when the all clear is sounded. I'm afraid the United States is not going to be an easy task. There are dead Americans, there are sick Americans. We will have to stay here at the fortress until we get word from the president that it is safe. I don't know, maybe two or three days. In the meantime, we have to prepare Zeppy Riley for a task that will definitely be laid before him. Forever laying the cornerstones for future nuclear nonproliferation and a worldwide disarmament movement and reaching out his hands and healing the injured world. One devastated nation at a time. *He is a musician of destiny! We'll have to just wait and watch!*"